RACING HEARTS

Lila turned on the sweetness in her voice. "Roger, I've seen the way you run. I bet you're faster than anyone in school." She batted her eyelashes as she gazed at him.

"You really think so?" Roger asked. His voice betrayed his nervousness at actually speaking to his dream girl.

"I bet you're even faster than Bruce Patman. And, Roger," Lila added, making her voice husky, "I'd love to see you beat *him*. You ought to enter the race."

"I can't." Roger heaved a deep sigh.

Lila widened her eyes in disbelief. "And I thought you were such a strong, forceful person. I'm disappointed in you."

In an instant Roger realized that right now he meant nothing to Lila, but if he ran and won, there was a chance of changing that.

"You're right, Lila," he said with conviction. "I should be in the race." He hopped over the wire fence and dashed toward the starting blocks.

Bantam Books in the Sweet Valley High Series
Ask your bookseller for the books you have missed

SWEET VALLEY HIGH

RACING HEARTS

Written by
Kate William

Created by
FRANCINE PASCAL

BANTAM BOOKS
TORONTO · NEW YORK · LONDON · SYDNEY · AUCKLAND

RL 7, IL age 12 and up

RACING HEARTS
A Bantam Book / June 1984

Sweet Valley High is a trademark of Francine Pascal

Conceived by Francine Pascal

Produced by Cloverdale Press Inc.,
133 Fifth Avenue, New York, N.Y. 10003

Cover art by James Mathewuse

ISBN 0-553-24131-1

Published simultaneously in the United States and Canada

Bantam Books are published by Bantam Books, Inc. Its trademark,
consisting of the words "Bantam Books" and the portrayal of a rooster,
is Registered in U.S. Patent and Trademark Office and in other
countries. Marca Registrada. Bantam Books, Inc., 666 Fifth Avenue,
New York, New York 10103.

PRINTED IN THE UNITED STATES OF AMERICA

O   0 9 8 7 6

To Debra Spector

One

"Jessica, I've been looking all over the house for you," Elizabeth Wakefield told her identical twin sister. "Mom wants you downstairs right away. She's making pancakes."

Jessica continued to stand before the full-length mirror in her parents' bedroom, admiring the way she looked in her mother's chocolate-brown suit. "I'll be down in a second. What do you think, Liz? I know brown's not my usual color, but I think it's a good color for business, don't you?"

Elizabeth sat down on her parents' king-size bed, eyeing her twin as if she were an alien who had just crawled out of a spaceship. The color *did* go well with Jessica's blond hair and tanned, flawless complexion, and the lines of the suit showed off the slender, shapely legs that were a mirror image of Elizabeth's own. But to say that Jessica wasn't the business-suit

1

type would have been the understatement of the decade.

"What's this all about?" Elizabeth asked. "Your role in the next school play?"

Elizabeth regretted her words as soon as they were out of her mouth. The week before, her twin had seen her world come tumbling down like a house of straw in a windstorm. Jessica had not only suffered the humiliation of losing surf champ Bill Chase to another girl, but she'd also discovered that the movie producer she'd been certain had come to watch her in the school play had barely even noticed her. It seemed he'd been scouting Bill instead. It wasn't so much that Jessica had cared about either Bill or a movie career, but the embarrassment of being shot down twice in one night was too much for even the self-assured Jessica to bear. Elizabeth couldn't remember ever seeing her twin so crushed, and now, she realized, her thoughtless remark had probably only made Jessica feel worse.

"Oh, Jess, I'm sorry," Elizabeth lamented instantly.

Jessica turned around as she took off the tailored jacket and flung it carelessly on the bed. "Sorry about what? My not going to Hollywood?" As if to emphasize her complete lack of interest, Jessica casually ran her slender fingers through her shoulder-length hair before unbuttoning her mother's cream-colored blouse.

"It's no big deal. I hear they're all a bunch of phonies anyway."

"Come on, Jess, you don't really mean that," Elizabeth said as she placed the jacket on a wooden hanger.

"Yes, I do," Jessica said, continuing to undress as she spoke. "I was thinking about it, Liz, and all the guy ever said was that he was offering Bill a screen test. I'll bet you anything they take him to L.A., stick a camera in front of his face, and send him home the same day. Sounds like a big waste of time to me." Jessica donned a pair of blue running shorts and matching tank top.

Elizabeth picked up the rest of her mother's suit and hung it back in the closet. "And what does that have to do with modeling Mom's clothes? You usually spend Sunday mornings between the sheets."

"Too excited to sleep this morning. I've got at *least* three hundred and thirty-seven things to do."

"But aren't you going to the beach with Cara?"

Jessica shook her head emphatically.

Elizabeth remained puzzled. Cara Walker was her sister's best friend. "What's the matter? You two have another fight?"

"No, sister dear. What I'm trying to tell you is that I'm no longer interested in spending idle hours in the sun gossiping with my girlfriends. It's *sooo* juvenile."

3

Elizabeth reached over and grabbed her sister's arm. "OK, Jess, what's up *now*?"

"I was going to tell you over breakfast, but I've decided it's time I stopped being so frivolous with my life. I should be thinking about the future."

Elizabeth stared at her sister in amazement. Was this really her twin who was saying these words? "Since when have you cared about life after high school?" Elizabeth questioned.

Jessica plopped down on the bed. "The more I thought about this Hollywood thing, the more I realized how little planning for the future I've actually done. Neither have most of my friends, for that matter. So I decided now is the time to begin," she said. "To get a head start on everyone else," she added in typical Jessica Wakefield fashion.

"Isn't this a bit sudden?" Elizabeth asked. "Last week you were ready to be an actress, now you say it's something else. How do you know you won't change your mind and forget it all as soon as you go outside and see what a nice day it is?"

Jessica brushed aside her sister's doubting words. "Look, Liz, sometimes an idea strikes you, and you just know it's the right thing to do. You're a perfect example. Didn't you just realize one day that you were going to be a writer?"

Elizabeth fell silent. She never talked much

about her writing to anyone, with the exception of Mr. Collins, the faculty adviser of *The Oracle*, Sweet Valley High's school newspaper. "It didn't exactly happen like that," Elizabeth said. "But *my* goal is beside the point. I just can't help wondering if this new focus on a career is only something to occupy your time while you're between boys."

"That's where you're dead wrong, Elizabeth Wakefield," Jessica said, flashing her sister a look of indignation. "I'm serious about this. I never said I was giving up boys. But I've got to think about other things, too. I've just come to realize there's more to life than drive-ins on Saturday nights and beach parties every Sunday afternoon."

Elizabeth was still dubious. It wasn't the first time she'd heard her sister resolve to change her ways. "All I can say is I'll believe it when I see it."

Jessica got up from the bed. "Thanks a lot, Elizabeth," she spat out angrily. "You know, I expected a little more encouragement from you. I thought you'd be thrilled that I'd finally decided to set some goals for myself. Isn't that what you've been trying to get me to do for ages?"

"Well, yes," Elizabeth admitted.

"So why can't you believe I'm ready to start?"

She didn't know how Jessica did it, but somehow Elizabeth had managed to wind up on the defensive once again. Nevertheless, there was something about the conviction she heard in Jessica's voice that made her willing to give her sister the benefit of the doubt. "I'm sorry, Jess. I guess I'm feeling a little like one of the townspeople in the story of the boy who cried wolf. But if you're serious and if there's anything I can do to help, just give a yell."

"Thanks. I knew I could count on you, Liz." Jessica hugged her sister impulsively. "Now, didn't you say something about a nice hot stack of pancakes?"

Elizabeth gasped. "Mom's going to kill us!" she cried. "The pancakes will be ice cold by now."

But Jessica knew better. Linking her arm through Elizabeth's, she slowly and calmly led her sister down the carpeted stairs. "I'll bet Mom waited." She inhaled deeply. "I don't smell a thing."

Jessica was right, Elizabeth noted as the two walked into the spacious, tiled kitchen. Her parents were sitting quietly at opposite ends of the table reading the newspaper and nursing their coffee. The batter, a special Wakefield family recipe, was on the counter next to the grill, waiting for the girls' arrival.

Not wanting to disturb her mother, who appeared totally caught up in the editorial section, Elizabeth began to make the pancakes herself. That's why she didn't see the expression on her parents' faces when Jessica dropped her bombshell.

"Daddy, I have a big favor to ask," Jessica said firmly. "I want an after-school job in your office. And I want to start tomorrow."

Two

"Do you believe this weather?" Lila Fowler complained bitterly the following morning.

Jessica took off her yellow rain slicker and shook it gently before hanging it up in her locker. The morning's sudden downpour had caught the weather forecasters by surprise, flooded the streets of Sweet Valley, and dampened a lot of spirits. Cara Walker was so convinced the rain would aggravate her budding cold that she'd decided to stay home that morning.

But Jessica wasn't disturbed. "Oh, Lila," she said, "don't tell me you're upset about a little water. Afraid it's going to make your hair frizz?"

"Jessica, sometimes you really get to me," Lila said, trying to straighten out her wavy brown hair with her fingers. "Just because your hair is frizzproof doesn't mean you can't have some sympathy for other people's problems."

Jessica gave Lila a once-over. Most girls would sell their soul to have Lila's problems, she thought. Wearing the latest designer blouse and a pair of jeans that outlined every inch of her trimly shaped legs, Lila was the envy of many girls at Sweet Valley High. Even the rain hadn't hurt, adding a fullness to her wavy hair that Jessica could seldom achieve with her curling iron. "You look great," Jessica told her. "Really, I don't think you have anything to worry about." She smiled slyly. "You're not trying to make a good impression on anyone in particular, are you?"

Lila returned the sly smile. Pretty and smart—not to mention the daughter of one of Sweet Valley's richest men—Lila was never lacking for male attention. But in her opinion, few of them were good enough for her. "No, I'm between boyfriends—just like you, Jessica." She couldn't resist getting in a dig.

Jessica directed her piercing aquamarine stare toward her friend. "If you think I'm upset over Bill Chase, you're wrong, Lila. I'm sure he and DeeDee will make a lovely couple."

"My, my, aren't we bighearted this morning. Are you sure the rain hasn't made your brain soggy?" Lila asked. "A week ago you weren't in such a forgiving mood."

"Well, that was then and this is now. Besides, what's wrong with wishing someone a little

9

happiness?" Jessica replied, her voice pure sweetness and light.

"Nothing. Nothing at all," Lila said. She was still unconvinced about Jessica's sincerity, but realizing she was getting nowhere, she changed the subject. "I wonder who we'll see at the Dairi Burger this afternoon."

"What makes you so sure I'll even be there?" Jessica asked.

"Where else would you go when it's too wet for the beach?"

"There are other places in Sweet Valley besides the Dairi Burger and the beach," Jessica reminded Lila.

"I see." Lila shook her head in that all-knowing way of hers. "You've already struck again. No wonder you're feeling so generous about Bill. Who's the lucky guy?"

"It has nothing to do with guys, Lila." Jessica took out her chemistry and French notebooks and slammed the door of her locker with her foot. "After school I begin my first day of work at my father's law office."

That was the last thing Lila had expected to hear. "Work? Why? Why on earth would you do that?"

"I know the concept of working is alien to you, Lila, but some people *do* enjoy it. I've decided I'd like to follow in my father's footsteps and become a lawyer, and there's no better time than now to start."

"But after school? What about your social life?"
Lila shook her head in disbelief.

"Dad's office closes at six. That still leaves plenty of time for my social life," Jessica explained. "Though I don't know how much dating I'll be doing for a while. I think I'd like to hold back until I see how the work goes."

Lila had to remind herself that this was Jessica she was talking to, not Elizabeth. "You're still going to the Bart dance next week, aren't you? I can't believe you'd want to miss that."

The dance was a big event on the Sweet Valley High social scene. It followed the annual running of the Barton Ames Memorial Mile, a very prestigious interscholastic race known informally as the Bart. "I'll be there," Jessica said. She began to walk slowly down the long corridor toward the classrooms. The hall was unusually messy, spotted with puddles and dirt brought in by rain-soaked students.

Lila avoided a streak of mud on the floor and fell in step beside Jessica. "I'll be there, too. But I'm not going to settle for just anyone."

"How about me, Lila?" asked Aaron Dallas, who came up behind them. The trio paused beside a row of lockers. "Didn't mean to eavesdrop, but I don't have a date yet and—"

"No, thanks, Aaron. I'm not *that* desperate," Lila teased. She gave the popular co-captain of the soccer team a playful shove. Lila had tried dating Aaron back in junior high, but there

11

hadn't been any chemistry. They had remained friends, however.

"Your loss, Lila," Aaron said good-naturedly. "Listen, I'd love to stay and talk, but I promised Bruce I'd go over our history assignment before class."

"Knowing Bruce Patman, he's probably going to make Aaron give him his homework," Jessica remarked caustically as Aaron walked off. She watched him as he disappeared down the corridor, swerving out of the way of Roger Barrett, who was running at full speed toward the locker area.

Lila snickered and pointed down the hallway. "Oops, don't look now, but here comes Bugs Bunny."

Just as Jessica caught sight of him, Roger stepped in a puddle and lost his footing. He slid about ten feet and landed on his backside on the wet floor, right in front of the girls. His books went flying in a semicircle around him, and his unfashionable, thick-framed glasses tilted at an odd angle on his square-jawed face.

It took all of Jessica's acting skills to hold back her giggles. The boy was a pathetic sight. His long legs stuck out of the cheap-looking jeans he wore, revealing his frayed white crew socks and well-worn sneakers. The force of his fall had caused his flannel shirt to open at the bottom, exposing a pale stomach that clearly hadn't seen the sun in years. As he got up, he

12

looked as if he couldn't decide whether to tend to his shirt first or to get his books before they were trampled by students on their way to class. His hesitation only heightened his clumsy appearance—and made Jessica's giggles harder to suppress.

Lila was only slightly more composed as she quipped, "Hey, what's up, doc?"

For the first time Roger noticed his audience. Lila Fowler was absolutely the last girl in the world he wanted to catch him off guard like this. He could feel his face flush with embarrassment, and he quickly closed his shirt and tucked it in. He'd had a crush on Lila for a very long time. Although he knew there was no chance of her caring about him, he'd never given up on the fantasy, even when he had heard her say at a party that she wouldn't dance with him "if he were the last boy on earth." He *still* always tried his best to impress her. This latest act, however, had done nothing to help his cause.

"Excuse me," he mumbled, turning away from her. He picked up his books as fast as he could and raced down the hall to his locker.

Once he was out of earshot, both Jessica and Lila let themselves go. "Do you believe him?" Lila finally sputtered. She'd been laughing so hard that tears had gathered in the corners of her eyes.

"I thought I was going to die," Jessica replied. "I couldn't have held it in too much longer."

"It would have served old Bugs right if we *had* laughed in his face," Lila said nastily.

"Hey, why do you call him Bugs Bunny, anyway?"

" 'Cause he *bugs* me," Lila explained as she and Jessica resumed their walk down the corridor. "The creep's had a crush on me forever, and I'm getting tired of it."

"Lila Fowler scorning the affections of an eligible bachelor?" Jessica said mockingly. Pretending to be serious, she continued. "It *is* getting late, you know. Maybe you ought to let *him* take you to the dance."

Lila sneered. "I'd rather date a fish." Once again she was overcome with giggles.

Jessica wasn't finished. "You're just saying that because he doesn't drive to school in a Ferrari."

"He doesn't drive anything, Jess. I don't even think he takes the school bus!"

Jessica was enjoying pleading Roger's case. When she became a lawyer, she'd have to defend plenty of lost causes like Roger Barrett, and there was no better time than now to begin sharpening her skills. "But, Lila, underneath the glasses and worn clothes is a boy who needs the kind of things a smart girl like you can teach him. Why don't you give the guy a break and go out with him? You know he wants you to."

"Jessica Wakefield, have you lost your mind?

If you think he's so great, go out with him yourself."

Jessica looked at her friend as if she'd suggested drinking Drano. The joke had gone far enough. It was one thing to defend Roger, quite another to date him. "No way, José," she said, wrinkling her nose in disgust.

Roger stuffed his books into his locker, cursing himself for losing control in front of Lila. *If only I hadn't slipped like that,* he thought, *maybe she wouldn't think I was such a fool.*

"You look like your cat just died."

Recognizing the voice, Roger turned around and smiled at Olivia Davidson, the arts editor for *The Oracle*, and one of his closest friends in school. "Hi, Liv," he said weakly.

"What's wrong?" Olivia asked.

"I just made a fool of myself in front of Lila Fowler."

"And that's why you have bags under your eyes?"

"Oh, that." Roger dismissed his tired expression with a shrug. "You'd have bags, too, if you were up till three in the morning studying."

"Not again." Olivia's voice was full of sympathy now. "How long is that going to go on, Roger?"

"Probably till I graduate—or at least until I truly understand trigonometry."

"Poor Roger."

Yeah, that's the problem: Roger is poor, he thought grimly. But he didn't want anyone, even Olivia, to know the truth—that he spent almost all of his after-school hours working as a janitor in a Sweet Valley office building. He'd gone to great pains to convince everyone that he spent all these afternoons studying. In truth, his studying was done when he should have been sleeping.

"Hey, I shouldn't be complaining. If I want to be a doctor, I've got to understand this stuff. I've got to get used to sleepless nights and be prepared to work hard."

Olivia shook her head, letting her untamed curls cascade around her narrow shoulders. "But not too hard," she insisted. "School's supposed to be fun, too."

Maybe for some people, he thought, *but not when your mother's too sick to hold a steady job and your father's too drunk.* "But what about you, Liv? You work pretty hard. When do you have time for play?"

"All the time. I mean, working at the museum and giving tours and lectures about the artists doesn't seem like work. That job is a dream come true for me—not to mention that it pays for the clothes on my back."

Roger eyed her carefully. "That's a new skirt, isn't it?" He wasn't sure he liked it, but it was in keeping with Olivia's offbeat sense of style.

16

Olivia proudly showed off the floral print skirt. It was so long it nearly covered her Chinese sandals. "The latest in chic from Martha's Thrift Shop. Goes well with the scarf, don't you think?" She fingered the long strip of faded silk tied loosely around her neck.

"Liv, when are you going to start shopping at the mall like everyone else around here?"

"What? And *be* like everyone else? That's not my style, Roger. I guess that's why I'm arts editor of *The Oracle* and not fashion editor. Speaking of which, I've got to hand my latest column in to Penny. See you later, Roger."

Olivia was already out of sight when the bell rang. Putting his legs into high gear, Roger ran up the stairs to his first class.

Three

Bruce Patman threw his towel against his cubicle in the boys' locker room in disgust. "I don't believe Coach Schultz, making us run in the rain." Droplets of water dripped from his dark hair onto his red and white Sweet Valley running shorts.

"Yeah, I'm glad we were playing inside," said John Pfeifer. He and Todd Wilkins had just finished a one-on-one game of basketball. "But I can understand why the coach would want you to be prepared for the Bart trials tomorrow."

"I hope the skies clear up by then," Bruce said. "Running in the muck is not my idea of a good time."

"Does that mean you're not going to try out for the race if it's raining?" As sports editor for *The Oracle*, John smelled a scoop here. For weeks Bruce had been bragging about how he was going to blow everybody away at the trials.

He'd even gone as far as working out with the track team in addition to running extra laps after school. If he didn't compete now, it would be big news.

"Of course I'm running," Bruce insisted. "I still aim to prove I'm the best athlete in school, certainly better than those clowns on the track team." He looked around quickly to make sure the guys he had just been training with were in the shower and safely out of earshot. "All I meant was that if the track is muddy, I'm not going to get a chance to break four minutes."

"As if you stand a chance of getting any where near four minutes," Todd interjected.

Bruce looked at the tall basketball player as if he were a worm. "Hey, Wilkins, you should talk. I don't hear anyone around here calling you speedy."

"At least I don't make any claims to be. You're the only one who seems to think you're a cinch to win the trials—not to mention coming out the big man in the Bart."

Todd wasn't usually so testy; in fact, he was one of the most easygoing students at Sweet Valley. But when he was pushed hard enough, his anger ran deep, and he still had good reason to hold a grudge against Bruce. The smooth-talking Bruce had tried to take advantage of Elizabeth Wakefield, Todd's girlfriend, when she'd been at her most vulnerable—after an accident that had left her acting completely out of character for several weeks. Fortunately, Bruce had failed. But only barely.

"Tell me, Wilkins, who do *you* think's going to win? Esteban? You know he's the school's distance runner only because no one else wanted to be. Riley? The guy's purely a sprinter. And no one else from the track team even has the guts to try out." Bruce sneered. "Face it, Wilkins, I'm our school's only hope. And I'm willing to wager I'm just as fast as those guys from the other schools. I plan to take home that trophy next Saturday."

"And I suppose it wouldn't bother you that you'd be depriving some guy of a college education if you win?" Todd was referring to the full scholarship to Sweet Valley College that went along with the trophy.

"Come off it, Wilkins. Nobody's run that race just for the scholarship in years."

"Have you made up your mind yet about whether to try out, Todd?" asked John.

"I'm still not sure. But I *could* use the scholarship—unlike some people in this room." Todd eyed Bruce coldly as he took off his soaked T-shirt. "I imagine I have as good a chance as anyone. These legs of mine do OK on the basketball court. What about you, John?" Todd asked.

"Nah, covering the race for *The Oracle* will keep me busy enough. Besides, scholarship or no scholarship, there's no way I'm going to subject myself to Coach Schultz's practices. That man's a killer."

"Maybe," Todd said as he headed toward the showers. "But he's one of the best coaches this school has ever had."

"Yeah, John, he's not so bad," put in Tony Esteban, who'd come in from the shower area just in time to hear Todd's comment, "if you happen to be a football player. He saves all his real coaching for them. When it comes to us runners, he's nothing but a drill sergeant."

"And you can bet he's going to make the guys who qualify for the race work their tails off," John added. "Nobody from Sweet Valley has won this race in years. He's hungry. You can see the fire in his eyes."

"That's not fire, John. It's fear," said Bruce. "If you ask me, I think the coach's days here as athletic director are numbered—and winning the race has nothing to do with it."

John whipped around and gave Bruce a fierce look. "What are you talking about, Patman?"

"Last week's school board meeting, that's what. My father said he never saw the coach so mad in his life. Seems the board turned down Schultz's request for more money—and he threatened to quit."

"I'd think even you could tell he was bluffing," John scoffed.

Bruce shook his head stubbornly. "No, I don't think so. I've never heard Dad say a word about

21

those meetings before, but he was pretty concerned when he came back this time. Take my word, guys, we may be seeing the coach's last hurrah."

Tony snorted. As a member of the track team, a team that had a far poorer record than any of the other ones at school, he'd been subjected to more of Coach Schultz's workouts and lectures than he cared to think about. "I say good riddance."

"Hey, Tony," John noted, "just because he made you do ten extra laps the other day doesn't mean he's not going to be missed."

"He doesn't have to coach track. He could hire someone else to do it. He should stick to football," Tony said stubbornly. "You're not going to see *me* working overtime for him and that race."

"Suit yourself," Bruce said. "That just makes my chances of winning that much better."

"Who cares?" Tony said. "I mean, if it were a long-distance race it would be a whole different story. But this isn't even my event. As far as I'm concerned, the best part about the Bart is the dance afterward."

"I'm with you on that," Bruce agreed. "As long as I win."

"Sure," John added. "So you can play the big hero role you do so well. Who're you going with?"

Bruce shrugged. "I haven't decided yet. What about you?"

"Oh, I don't know. Annie Whitman maybe."

The boys let out a chorus of whistles. "Have you made an appointment?" Tony questioned. "I've heard she's booked up for weeks and isn't going to quit until she's had a go at every guy in school."

"She's well on her way," Bruce noted. "Charlie Cashman took her up to Miller's Point on Saturday, and from the way he looked yesterday when I ran into him, all I can say is that he must have had a *very* good time."

"How about you, Bruce? She going to get a chance to work her magic on you?" Tony asked.

Bruce smiled slyly. "Only if she's lucky."

Jessica strode confidently into her father's law office that afternoon. "Hi, Mrs. Kelly, is my father in?"

"He's on the phone right now," the receptionist said, looking down at her telephone console. "He asked me to tell you to have a seat and make yourself comfortable."

"Fine," Jessica said cheerfully, settling down on one of the gray velvet couches in the waiting area.

She took a magazine from the glass coffee table and began to leaf through the pages, but she could concentrate only on the wonderful experience that lay ahead of her. She was glad she'd decided to become a lawyer. Law was an exciting field to be in these days, she reflected, especially for a woman. For a second she thought of Joyce Davenport, the public defender on "Hill Street Blues." Now there was someone Jessica could admire. Glamorous, dedicated to her career, upholding the rights of others, yet still making time for romance. *That's the kind of lawyer I'd like to be*, Jessica thought, though a second later she discarded the notion. It was one thing to defend lost causes but quite another to have to defend really grizzly, dangerous criminals. Civil law, something more along the lines of her father's practice, was much better, she concluded. Conferring with other lawyers— including lots of handsome men—certainly had to be at least as exciting, and a lot less dangerous.

She wondered what case her father would have her work on first. She found herself relishing the prospect of working by his side, helping him prepare his clients' defenses. He spent a good deal of time at the county courthouse, and Jessica couldn't wait for her father to take her down there with him. From dinner-table conversation she recalled that one of the cases he was handling concerned someone who was suing George Fowler, Lila's father. The Fowlers had trod upon many helpless citizens of the town over the years, and her father was among a growing number of residents who were beginning to stand up and fight against the Fowler power. She'd volunteer to help on that one. She thought gleefully about the prospect of being able to give the man what he had coming to him, not to mention gloating over her father's victory in front of Lila. Even though they were friends, there was an unspoken rivalry between the two of them.

Just then her father appeared, interrupting Jessica's thoughts. "Well, Jessica, are you ready to start?" He was smiling proudly.

Ned Wakefield had always hoped one of his children would take an interest in law, but never in his wildest dreams had he thought it would be Jessica. Delight shone in his face as his daughter smiled up at him and nodded. "Come along with me, honey," he said.

Jessica rose and followed her father. She was surprised when they didn't turn left down the short hall to his office but instead headed straight to the utility room in the back of the suite. "Jess," her father said, walking into the brightly lit room, "I don't think you've met my new office manager, Trudy Roman. She'll explain what needs to be done around here. Trudy, this is my daughter Jessica. I've got a lot of work to do, so I'll leave the two of you alone. Enjoy yourself, Jess, and if you have any questions, don't hesitate to speak up. Not that I've ever known you to stay silent when something was on your mind," he added with a smile. He closed the door behind him as he left.

Jessica looked around the room. She'd hardly noticed it the few times she'd been up to her father's office in the past. Not that there was much worth noticing. One wall was lined with gray steel shelving filled with various office supplies and papers. On the other side of the room was a copying machine, and on a low table next to it was a big computer.

Trudy approached her with a stack of papers several inches thick. "Jessica, I want four copies of each of these documents, collated and stapled," she announced in a clipped, nononsense voice.

"What are they?" Jessica asked.

"Legal briefs," she responded. "Your father needs them right away. You know how to work a copying machine, don't you?"

"Oh, sure," Jessica said confidently. "There's nothing to it."

"Good," Trudy said. "I've got things to do in the outer offices, so you'll be on your own here. I'll be in the conference room if you need me."

Jessica sighed as she began to feed the papers into the machine. She wondered if Joyce Davenport had started in the copy room. Although Jessica had never operated her father's copier before, she'd run off dozens of copies of cheers on a similar machine in the principal's office. The work was monotonous, and after about five minutes of it she was ready to climb the walls. This wasn't the kind of job she'd bargained for. Looking around the room, she discovered a portable radio on one of the shelves and tuned it to the local rock station. At least the music would help relieve the dreariness.

Not for long. Less than a minute later Trudy marched into the office. "What do you think you're doing, Miss Wakefield?"

"Making copies, as you wanted," Jessica said, not bothering to hide her boredom.

Trudy clicked off the radio. "Not with that noise machine you're not. Your father asked me to come in here and remind you that this is an office, not a disco," she proclaimed. "I suggest you get back to work."

"Battle-ax," Jessica hissed after Trudy closed the door behind her. How dare that woman order her around? Jessica wondered what act of desperation had made her father hire this tyrant.

It took her nearly an hour and a half to finish her assignment. Before giving them to Trudy, however, Jessica decided to take a look at some of the documents she'd been copying, figuring that was how her father expected her to learn. From the wording at the top, they appeared to have something to do with real estate, though even after she began reading, Jessica wasn't exactly sure. The documents were in English—sort of—but the language was so convoluted that it was beginning to give her a headache. It made for even duller reading than her chemistry text.

This was law? she thought. Where was the excitement of court cases, the challenge of defending the people that her father was always talking about? This was no fun at all. The realization, coupled with the thought of having to be at Trudy's constant beck and call, suddenly made the thought of spending another day in that office unbearable.

She carried the stack of documents into the conference room. "I've finished," she told Trudy. "Now what?"

"Go to the office-supplies store downstairs and get another box of these forms." Opening up one of the files on the table, she handed Jessica a standard legal form.

Jessica took her time walking down the narrow hallway to the elevator. She didn't think her father would be too proud of her when she told him she'd had enough of this job after only one day. While waiting for the elevator to arrive, she began to think how she could break the news to him. She was sure she'd come up with a plausible excuse. She always did.

"You new here?"

Lost in her scheming, Jessica was startled by a voice. She turned around to see where it came from—and definitely liked what she saw. Over six feet tall, with wavy golden hair and smiling brown eyes, the boy who'd asked the question was leaning lazily against the wall. "What makes you think I work here?" she asked.

"No pocketbook," he said, moving closer. "I don't know of any girl who'd be walking around here without a pocketbook unless she had it stashed away somewhere in an office drawer."

"How do you know so much about feminine habits?" she asked. "Or do *you* keep a pocketbook hidden away, too?"

He laughed. "When you work in an office, you notice those things," he said just as the elevator arrived. Graciously he held out his arm. "After you, um . . ."

"Jessica," she said, stepping inside. "Jessica Wakefield."

"Not *the* Jessica Wakefield," he said. "Daughter of Ned Wakefield, attorney at law?"

"So you read office signs. I'm impressed," Jessica said, a teasing note in her voice. Working in her father's office might have its rewards after all. Already she was beginning to feel a tingle of excitement at the prospect of being in this boy's arms. But she didn't want him to know that—at least not until she had enough time to gauge his interest. Adjusting her tone slightly, she asked politely, "And you are—?"

He extended a hand. "Dennis Creighton. I work part-time at my dad's ad agency across the hall from your father. How come I haven't seen you around here before?"

"Today's my first day on the job." *And my*

last, she thought. But something made her hold back that information. It was the glint in Dennis's eyes. She'd seen that look too many times not to realize that it meant he was clearly taken with her. *So far, so good*, she thought, her own attraction mounting with each passing moment. A guy like Dennis could even be enough of a lure to make her want to stay on the job just a little while longer. "I'm on my way to the office-supplies store," she told him, holding out the form in her hand.

The glint in Dennis's eyes worked its way down to his mouth, where a small smile was taking shape. "And how does it feel to be a working woman?" he asked. "Training for the secretarial life?"

"Oh, no," Jessica said, letting the fire from her blue-green eyes emphasize her words. "I'm planning to be a lawyer."

Dennis was definitely impressed. "Just what I like, a girl with ambition," he said as they arrived at the main floor. "I hate girls who think planning ahead means picking out a new bathing suit to wear to the beach the next weekend."

"I know what you mean," Jessica said, rolling her eyes meaningfully as she stepped out of the elevator. "I know too many girls like that, and the only people they interest are themselves." She didn't hesitate to add, "Of course I never pay any attention to them." She didn't want Dennis to think even for a moment that she might be that kind of girl.

Dennis followed her out of the elevator. "No, I wouldn't think a girl like you would have to waste her time on such trivial things—especially now that you're working. How do you like your new job?"

"It's wonderful," Jessica lied. "I'm so lucky my father's giving me this opportunity to be here."

"Yeah, fathers are good for that," Dennis agreed.

Jessica turned her head back slightly as she continued to walk toward the store. "So how come I've never seen you around school?"

"Maybe you haven't been looking closely enough," he said in a husky voice.

"No, I pretty much know everyone at Sweet Valley High. Oh, I know. You go to the college, right? I don't know too many people there except for my sister's friend Enid's boyfriend. George Warren. Know him?" There was a time when Jessica might have fibbed and said she went to Sweet Valley College if she felt it might make a good impression. But lying about her age had once gotten her into big trouble with a boy, and she wasn't about to make that mistake again. It was one of the few areas where she believed that honesty was the best policy.

Dennis seemed to hesitate a moment before answering. "I'm not in college. I go to El Carro."

"Oh, a rival, huh?" Jessica taunted as she gave Dennis a slow, careful once-over.

Dennis studied the expression in Jessica's aquamarine eyes as he tried to determine if he'd won her approval. "I'll tell you this much. I *wish* I went to Sweet Valley."

"Well, I'm not going anywhere if I don't get these forms," she said breezily. "See you around sometime." She moved away from him toward the store.

"Yeah," Dennis said, admiring Jessica's back, adding under his breath, "you can count on it."

Four

The rain had passed through Sweet Valley, leaving a sparkly clear horizon and pleasantly warm weather the following morning. It was a perfect day for the race trials, and everyone was excused from first-period class to cheer on the participants.

Shading her eyes from the sun, Cara Walker peered out at the track. "I see Mark and Peter and Tony, but where's Bruce?"

"You know Bruce," Lila said dryly. "He's probably waiting to make his grand entrance. It wouldn't surprise me if he bought himself a new running outfit just for this."

"Custom-made, I suppose," Jessica said, a trace of sarcasm in her voice. She once had been involved with Bruce, and the aftermath of the affair still left a bitter taste in her mouth.

"So how's the law business?" Lila asked. "Defend anyone interesting yesterday?"

"Don't patronize me, Lila. As it happens, it was one of the most exciting afternoons I'd had in a long time."

"Oh, yeah?" Lila probed. "What's his name?"

For a split second Jessica looked surprised. Were her feelings that transparent? But then she realized that the remark was just Lila's way of indicating she didn't take Jessica's interest in law too seriously. "His name is Ned Wakefield," Jessica shot back. "And thanks to him, I had a very enlightening afternoon."

"Look, guys, there he is," Cara interrupted, pointing toward the field.

"Looks like you were right, Lila," Cara said. "Mr. Big strikes again."

With an arrogance born of years of practice, Bruce Patman strutted slowly out of the dressing area and onto the track. His brand-new red running shorts were short enough to expose nearly the entire length of his long, muscled legs, while his white, sleeveless T-shirt emphasized his sleek, tanned arms. He had the look of a winner, and with the utmost confidence, he warmed up as the crowd continued to grow.

Elizabeth Wakefield, sitting on the bench below her sister, paid scant attention to Bruce. Her mind was on Todd, and she scanned the stadium seats looking for him. "Where could he be?" she asked Enid Rollins, her best friend.

"I saw him this morning. I imagine he'll be

here any second," Enid said. "He knows you're sitting here, doesn't he?"

"We had it all arranged," Elizabeth said. She turned and looked behind her and saw Olivia Davidson walking down the bleacher steps with Roger. She marveled at the way Olivia seemed to glide effortlessly without tripping over her long skirt.

Olivia acknowledged Elizabeth's smile and sat down on the bench below her. "Hi, Elizabeth. I was sitting in the *Oracle* office, trying my best to avoid this spectacle, when this fellow over here abducted me." She pointed to Roger, who was now staring intently at the track. Sensing that something was bothering him, Olivia gave him a little tap. "Hey, Roger, are you with us?"

Roger turned around slowly. Elizabeth thought she spotted a look of wistfulness on his face. "You want to be out there, don't you, Roger?" she asked gently.

Too quickly, Roger responded, "Not me. Who'd want to be parading around in underwear in front of all these people?"

"Only someone who might want to prove he's the fastest runner in school," Elizabeth challenged.

"Bruce Patman, you mean," Roger said.

"I'm talking about you, Roger. You spend every afternoon running out of this place at breakneck speed. I can't believe you're not the

35

least bit curious about how you'd rank next to those guys. Why aren't you out there?"

"I told you," Roger said, his voice rising slightly. "I'm not interested in this stuff." He was not only miffed that Elizabeth had mentioned his running, he was afraid she might force him to reveal the real reason he couldn't participate in the race. Outside of his family, Elizabeth was the only person who knew about his job—a job he couldn't afford to risk losing simply to run this race.

"And why should he be?" Olivia questioned. "Roger's never run in a race in his life."

"Maybe he ought to start. The first prize in the Bart is a scholarship to Sweet Valley College," Elizabeth pointed out.

Olivia grew quiet. While she was unaware of Roger's job, it was painfully obvious by his wardrobe that he could really use the scholarship. "Roger, maybe you ought to listen to Elizabeth," she prodded.

"She doesn't know what she's talking about," Roger said, his anger evident in the tight lines that had formed around his mouth. "The subject is closed. I'm not going to run in this race!"

But Elizabeth wasn't through. "I think you're making a big mistake. . . ."

Lila overheard the conversation and was amused. "What's with your sister?" she whispered to Jessica. "How come she wants to see Bugs Bunny run?"

"Beats me," Jessica said, her mind on how she could arrange to meet Dennis again. She'd left him rather abruptly the day before, hoping that she'd left him wanting more. But just in case she was wrong, she decided she'd better plan a way to ensure there'd be a second chance to attract him.

"Well, watch this," Lila said as an idea popped into her head. Rising so he could see her, Lila called out, "Hey, Roger, may I talk to you?"

At first Roger didn't react. But Jessica did, looking at Lila as if she were more than just a little crazy. "What are you trying to do?"

"Just adding a little fun to the proceedings." Lila smiled mysteriously. Then she called out a little louder, "Roger Barrett, would you please turn around?"

It's impossible, he thought. *Lila Fowler can't mean me. Not after yesterday.* Finally Elizabeth nudged him. "I think Lila wants your attention."

As soon as he looked up at her, Lila turned on the sweetness. "I don't mean to butt into your business, but I couldn't help overhearing your conversation. I think Liz is right, Roger. You ought to be out there."

Roger still couldn't believe his ears. "Why?" he asked her.

Lila batted her eyelashes as she gazed at him. "I've seen the way you run around campus. You're fast. I bet you're faster than anyone in school."

37

"You really think so?" he wondered. His voice rose about an octave on the last word, betraying his nervousness at actually speaking to his dream girl.

But if Lila noticed, she didn't seem to care. "I've had my eye on you," she went on, "and I'd bet you're even faster than Bruce Patman. And, Roger," she said, making her voice husky, "I'd love to see you beat him."

"I can't," Roger said.

"You mean you're afraid to find out?" Lila challenged him.

Roger shook his head. "You don't understand. It's nothing like that at all."

His stubbornness surprised her, but she wasn't ready to give up. "Prove it," she demanded.

"I can't." He heaved a deep sigh.

Lila widened her eyes in disbelief. "You *are* afraid, Roger. And here I thought you were such a strong, forceful person. I'm disappointed in you, really and truly disappointed." Clucking sadly, she made a big show of her disapproval by sitting down and pretending to pout.

"Lila, wait!" he shouted. It didn't take long for Roger to make up his mind. He had everything to gain and nothing to lose by getting on the field that day. At the moment he meant nothing to Lila, but if he ran and won, or ran and at least beat Bruce Patman, there was a chance of changing that. He wouldn't have to run in the final race and risk his job; but if he had the honor of placing in the trials, it might help open Lila's eyes.

"You're right, Lila," he said, standing. "I should be in the race."

He raced down the bleacher steps, hopped over the short wire fence in front of the stands, and jogged over to Coach Schultz. "I'd like to run, sir," he announced.

Surprised by the late entry, the coach took off his cap and scratched his head. "That your running outfit, boy?"

Roger looked down at his faded army fatigue pants and red T-shirt. His decision had come so fast, he hadn't stopped to think about his clothing. The race was going to start any minute now, and there wasn't time for him to change into his gym shorts. But at least he was wearing his only pair of sneakers. "I'm ready," Roger announced. "Where do I go?"

Coach Schultz chuckled. Having had Roger as a student in gym class, he was well aware of his ability to run. On more than one occasion, he had attempted to get Roger to try out for the track team but had stopped pursuing the issue after Roger's repeated refusals. He wasn't sure why the boy was interested in running now, but the coach wasn't about to discourage him. "Take your mark in lane three, next to Patman," Coach Schultz said, pointing to the oval. "The race starts in five minutes."

Roger smiled. "Thanks, Coach. I won't let you down."

"I know you won't," he said. "Good luck."

Back in the stands, Lila finally let out the laughter she'd been suppressing during her entire conversation with Roger. "Do you believe that guy?" she commented to Jessica and Cara. "I can't wait to see old Bugs make a fool of himself."

The girls joined in her laughter. "God, Lila, have you ever thought about becoming an actress?" Cara asked. "That was one of the finest con jobs I've seen in a long time. You even had me convinced there for a while."

"When you're on, you're on," Lila said, obviously proud of herself.

"Yeah, well your boyfriend stands as much chance of beating Bruce as I have of getting an A in chemistry," Jessica said.

Lila turned serious. "Don't call that nerd my boyfriend," she hissed. "Someone might believe you."

"I don't know, Lila," Jessica continued. "Maybe Liz ought to put in a few lines about you two in 'Eyes and Ears.' " She was referring to the gossip column her sister wrote for the school paper. "I think you'd make a lovely couple."

"That's enough, Wakefield," Lila said, her eyes shooting pure venom now. "It's just a joke, remember?"

Lila's words made Olivia's stomach churn.

Perhaps more than anyone else, she knew how much Roger liked Lila and how hurt he'd be to find out that her interest in him was a sham. But Olivia was unable to raise her voice against the popular girl. Though Olivia was well liked by most of her classmates, Lila looked upon her and her unconventional ways with disdain, and Olivia knew that Lila wouldn't take anything she said seriously.

But Elizabeth had also heard enough from Lila, and she had no qualms about criticizing her. "You're cruel, Lila," she said, her normally pleasant voice taking on a sharp edge. "That guy really likes you."

"Hey, I was only trying to do him a favor. Seems to me you were begging him to get out there and weren't getting anywhere. Maybe you're just jealous I've succeeded where you failed?"

"That's not what I'm talking about, and you know it," Elizabeth went on. "The only reason he's out there now is because of you. What's going to happen when he gets off the field and finds out you were laughing at him all this time?"

"You're being too sensitive, Liz. Roger knows there can never be anything between us. We have nothing in common."

That was certainly true, Elizabeth thought. Roger had integrity, compassion, and warmth, and all Lila had was a pretty face and a fat

41

charge account. But she left that unsaid. "Maybe I *am* being sensitive, Lila," she said, "because I know Roger, and you don't. But the one thing I'm glad about is that he's out there running. If I'm right, he's going to blow everyone off the field."

"Hey, Liz, how come you've become Roger's one-person rooting section?" Jessica asked.

"Because I believe in him, Jess."

"Well, what about Todd?"

"What about him?" Elizabeth wondered.

"Don't you believe in him, too? Or have you suddenly switched allegiance?"

"What *are* you talking about, little sister?" Elizabeth said in the exasperated tone she reserved for the times she lost patience with Jessica. She was only four minutes older than her sister, but at times like this she felt those minutes were more like years. "You know that nothing could come between Todd and me."

"So how come you're not cheering for him?" Jessica wanted to know. She pointed to the field.

This time it was Elizabeth's turn to be surprised. She followed her sister's gaze to the track, where Todd was doing warm-ups. Dressed in gym shorts and running shoes, he was obviously going to compete in the trials. Elizabeth stared at him openmouthed. "What's he doing there?"

"You mean you didn't know?" Jessica asked.

Something peculiar is going on here, Elizabeth thought. Although Todd was a fine basketball player, he had never before expressed much interest in running, let alone in this race. Her curiosity mounting, she continued to stare at him as he took his mark along with the other contestants.

Five

"Well, well, what do we have here?" Bruce Patman eyed Roger disdainfully. "I think you made a wrong turn, Roger. The freak show's at the circus down at the civic center."

Roger didn't answer, but took his place ahead of Bruce in the adjoining lane. Because it was to be a mile race, the runners would be making a staggered start. The longer he remained silent, the more Bruce teased him.

"This is a race for runners, not for water boys. Who said you could be out here?" Bruce turned to Mark Riley the captain of the track team. "Do you believe this, Mark?" he called out. "I guess this is what they mean by equal opportunity. Even bozos get to race."

Roger still said nothing. In a way he was glad Bruce was making fun of him. It gave him even more of a reason to try his best. This wasn't the first time Bruce had treated him this way—once

44

he'd told Roger that the sweat shirt he wore in gym was so old it belonged in a museum—and he was sure it wasn't going to be the last time either.

"Hey, Roger, haven't you heard of running shorts?" Bruce went on. "Or are you embarrassed to show off your legs?"

"Patman, cut it out," Todd snapped from his lane. "We've all heard enough."

Bruce was in no mood for a lecture. "Look, Wilkins, this is none of your business. If the guy's heard enough, let him speak up for himself."

But as far as Roger was concerned, Bruce could talk till he got blue in the face. All he was doing was sapping his own strength.

On the sidelines, Coach Schultz paced back and forth, looking over the field. He had some good runners out there, but he was clearly worried. Having scouted some of the top runners from the other schools' track teams, he knew the boys from Sweet Valley were in for tough competition. No one from the school had won this race since 1956.

Elizabeth said to Enid, "Take a look at Coach Schultz. You'd think somebody died."

Enid nodded, her hair blowing across her forehead. "You'd look pretty grim, too, if your job was on the line."

"What do you mean?"

"Winston Egbert told me he'd heard the coach

got chewed out by the school board last week. He thinks they might give Coach Horner the job of athletic director if no one from Sweet Valley places in the Bart."

"I don't believe it," Elizabeth said. As the author of the "Eyes and Ears" column, she usually kept a pretty close watch on happenings around the school, but this was news to her. "How could they do that? Coach Schultz is an institution."

"Even institutions can crumble," Enid noted. "You have to admit the guy is getting old. Could be they want new blood around here."

"I've got to check into this. Maybe John Pfeifer's heard something."

"It'll have to wait," Enid said, noticing the coach approaching the microphone set up next to the starting point. "I think the race is about to begin."

"Good morning, students and faculty." Coach Schultz's deep baritone pierced the air. All conversation seemed to stop at once. "Welcome to the trials for this year's Barton Ames Memorial Mile. As you know, this race honors a very fine young man who died before his time, a young man who loved to run as much as he loved life itself. His parents founded this race to give other young men a chance at bettering their lives. The winner and two runners-up of today's race will go on to the finals next week, competing with some of the area's top athletes for the first-prize trophy and scholarship to Sweet Valley College. It's my privilege now to introduce to you the boys who are competing this morning. In lane one we have Mark Riley; lane two, Bruce Patman; lane three, Roger Barrett; lane four, Todd Wilkins; lane five, Peter Sorley; lane six, Tony Estcban. May the best man win. Runners take your mark . . . get set—" Coach Schultz gave a short, shrill blast on his silver whistle, and the six boys took off.

Like a jackrabbit, Bruce Patman shot to the front of the pack and took the lead, snickering visibly as he passed Roger in the lane next to his. Mark sped up behind him, a close second, followed by Tony, Todd, and Peter, with Roger pacing himself behind them all.

Lila chuckled. "Look at old Bugs. It'll be a miracle if he makes it around even once."

Right below her, Elizabeth looked at the field with mixed emotions. Naturally she was rooting for her boyfriend, but it was almost as important to her that Roger place as well. She wasn't sure why Todd was out there, but of all of them Roger needed the scholarship most. It would be nice, she thought, if he and Todd could tie for first.

But at this point it didn't look as if either one would even qualify. Bruce Patman was way in front, striding like a gazelle, a picture-perfect example of high-speed running. His nearest competitor, Mark Riley, was a good ten paces behind, and the strain of the race was already showing on his lean, narrow face. The others were trailing, and as they reached the half-mile point, they were stretched single file in a curve that spanned a full quarter of the track.

Bruce was supremely confident as he looked back and surveyed the field. He was an expert runner who would have been the star miler on the track team if the schedule hadn't interfered with his first love, tennis. There was no way anyone could beat him now, he felt. Mark's specialty was the 440; so it was doubtful he'd finish with a spurt, and none of the others was nearly as fast. Even Tony Esteban didn't stand to catch him. At this point Tony was third, and even though he was known for coming on strong at the end, he was so far behind Bruce that he'd have to run his best time ever to beat him. Besides, Tony's strong point was his stamina in races far longer than this one. He was racing more because of pressure from Coach Schultz than because he thought he would win. Todd, Peter, and Roger were unknown quantities, but they didn't look as if they posed any threat.

But as they were approaching the three-quarter mark, Roger began to pick up ground, passing Peter and Todd. He was running faster, his speed pushing his straight hair off his face. His arms and legs were working now with the precision of a locomotive engine, pumping ever harder as he circled the track and closed in on the leaders.

It wasn't long before he passed Mark Riley, who was tiring and beginning to slow down noticeably. Then he passed Tony. That left only Bruce. But Bruce's advantage only coaxed Roger to move faster. Using all the power he had within, he stepped up his already lightning-quick gait. For every stride Bruce took, Roger was now taking two.

His progress didn't go unnoticed in the stands, and several crowd members began to chant his name and root him on. The loudest cheers came from Olivia, who was thrilled to see Roger finally get the attention he deserved. She was proud of him, as proud as any girlfriend would be. Even though their relationship was purely one of friendship, Olivia hadn't given up hope that someday Roger would notice the romantic side of her. There were a couple of times in the past when she felt he'd come close to asking her out, but he always seemed to back away as if he'd lost his courage. Maybe, she thought, this race, no matter what its outcome, would build up his confidence. She couldn't wait to find out.

Lila, who hadn't bothered to pay much attention to the race up to this point, suddenly began to take notice as Cara reached over to tug at her arm. "Look at Bugs go! Do you believe it?"

"What Bugs?" Jessica asked rhetorically. "He

looks more like Speedy Gonzales now." The newfound reverence in her voice was unmistakable. "He's fantastic, Lila. Kind of sheds new light on things, doesn't it?"

"What do you mean?" Lila asked.

"Do I have to spell it out for you? The boy who wins this race is going to be pretty popular around here. It wouldn't hurt to be seen with him."

"You can't be serious, Jessica."

"Why not? Have you ever really looked at Roger? He's not so bad-looking. So what if his taste in clothing leaves something to be desired? Nobody's perfect."

The race now appeared to be Roger's for the taking. Even Coach Schultz, who thought he knew how fast Roger was, let his silver whistle drop from his mouth as he stared in astonishment at the boy. Roger caught up with Bruce as they rounded the final turn. Bruce was so shocked to find someone at his side that he almost stopped dead in his tracks. A large part of the stadium was now rooting for the underdog, shouting, "Roger! Roger! Roger!"—which only added to Roger's momentum. Bruce's earlier optimism was gone, and even as he struggled to keep his pace, he knew the race was not going to be his. Roger quickened his steps, put in a final burst of speed, and crossed the finish line several seconds ahead of Bruce.

The crowd went wild, the cheering and stamping reverberating throughout the entire campus. Olivia and Elizabeth hugged each other in happiness, while Jessica, Lila, and Cara began to join the others who were heading toward the field.

The stunned boy didn't know how to react. Panting heavily, he looked back at the crowd blankly, wondering what to do next. Bruce slipped across the finish line in second place, his head bent in anger and disappointment, and turned toward the locker room without congratulating the winner. The other racers were more gallant, however, and showered their congratulations on Roger, eventually hoisting him on their shoulders way above the approaching crowd.

As his shock faded, Roger began to enjoy the glory, waving his appreciation to his fellow classmates. For the first time in his school career, he felt like a somebody, and he wanted to take advantage of the attention for as long as possible. It was as if he felt that at any moment it would all disappear.

Right after the boys lowered him back down to the ground, someone grabbed him and began to hug him tightly. The slender arms and wavy, light brown hair belonged to a girl, but at first he didn't know who it was.

"Roger, you were unbelievable!" she shouted. The voice was familiar. Could it be? "I've never seen anyone run so well. You were great!"

She loosened her arms a little, and Roger confirmed the fact that he was being showered with affection by the girl of his dreams. "Lila," he said with disbelief. "You're here. You're really here!"

"Where else would I be, Roger?" she said teasingly. "I told you I wanted to see you run. You didn't think I'd miss being at the finish line, did you?"

"Well, no," he said, groping for words. "I—I guess the whole thing is still like a dream to me."

"Then it's time to wake up, Roger. 'Cause I'm very much alive and here." Taking hold of a strand of his hair, she brushed it gently behind his ear, letting her fingers tickle his lobe enticingly for a brief moment.

Roger was speechless. Meanwhile, the crowd around him swelled. "Well, I'd better leave you to the rest of your fans. See you around, Rog." Lila blew him a kiss and then disappeared into the crowd.

Roger didn't have time to think about her as he was overwhelmed by well-wishers. Another girl hugged him, but this time the touch suggested only friendship. "Congratulations, Roger," Elizabeth said. "I knew you could do it."

"Thanks for having faith in me," he answered. "It helped to know there were a few people out there pulling for me."

"A few? Didn't you hear the crowd? You had the whole school behind you."

"Really? I figured there were a lot of people who wanted Bruce to win."

"Believe me, there were plenty more who wanted to see him lose. Face it, Roger, you're a hero."

"Do you know anyone around here who gives hero lessons? I've never played the part before."

"Just be yourself. The rest will come naturally."

Coach Schultz caught Elizabeth's words as he gave the star runner a big bear hug. "Natural, you bet. My boy, that was the best piece of running I've seen since Jack Ralston won the Bart in fifty-six."

"Thank you, Coach."

"Thank you nothing. The thanks are all mine, my boy. You knew what you were doing from the word go. Keeping behind all those others, pacing yourself for the final stretch. I'm very proud of you, Roger. Why, just imagine what you're going to do when we put real running clothes on you. Of course, you've got to realize that your natural abilities will only take you so far. You've got some strong competition in the Bart, and from now until the race I plan to run you, Bruce, and Tony hard. That's my style, you know, and it's worked well for me. Unfortunately, I haven't had the talent to work with in recent years, but you boys are just what the doctor ordered. I'll see you out here at two-thirty sharp."

Two-thirty. That was the time he was due at work! All the excitement faded as Roger came crashing down to earth. He couldn't afford to take time off to run, let alone hours every day for practice. Jobs for teens in Sweet Valley were hard to come by, and more than once his employer had told him how lucky Roger was to have his job, especially since it now paid him fifty cents an hour over the minimum wage.

He had to tell the coach he couldn't run. "Coach Schultz—" he began tentatively.

The coach turned around. "No excuses, Roger. Practice is a must, and I'm not going to let anyone get out of it. Even a speedster like you."

"But, Coach, I—"

Coach Schultz gave Roger the once-over. "Listen, don't worry about a uniform. I won't let anyone from Sweet Valley go without. I'll have some racing shorts ordered for you. In the meantime, you can practice in your gym outfit."

"But, Coach . . ."

Coach Schultz had already begun to walk off the field, having said all he intended to.

Well, Roger thought, at least he could savor the victory while it lasted. He'd be a nobody again by two-thirty that afternoon. Pasting a smile back on his face, he approached Olivia, who was still sitting in the stadium bleachers, her note pad in hand. She appeared to be lost in whatever she was writing. The happiness she'd felt at Roger's victory had faded quickly when she saw Lila make her play for him, and she was writing about her feelings.

"Hey, got some time for an old war-horse?" he asked, tapping her lightly on the arm. "Some race, huh?"

Olivia looked up. "Congratulations," she said politely. Closing her notebook, she rose, lifted her long skirt, and retreated back toward the campus.

Roger knew that Olivia wasn't much of a sports fan, but he expected more thanks from his good friend. Shaking his head, both at her behavior and at his own hopeless predicament, he walked toward the locker room.

Six

As the day went on, Roger grew more accustomed to his role as Sweet Valley sports hero. He would miss all the fuss when he was back to his normal routine. After he'd showered and gotten back into the same clothes he had worn during the race, he grabbed his books from his gym locker and headed for his American history class. But before he could get past the administration offices, he was stopped by Sweet Valley's principal, Mr. Cooper.

"We're mighty proud of you, Roger," Mr. Cooper said excitedly, throwing his arm around the startled boy. It had been a long time since Roger had seen the man known around school as Chrome Dome, and he had forgotten how accurate the nickname really was. Mr. Cooper's scalp shone like a car fender. The rumor was that he oiled his bald head, but it had never been proven. "Come with me, boy," Mr. Cooper continued, leading Roger into the administration office suite.

Smiling modestly, Roger took a seat on Mr. Cooper's plush green couch. Right in the middle of the principal's wooden desk was the microphone from which he made his daily announcements about school activities, rules, and anything else that came to his mind. "I'm going to be late for class," Roger said.

"No need to worry about that, Roger. I just had to call you in here to congratulate you. Why, do you know how fast you ran?" the principal asked, resting himself on the edge of his desk.

"No, sir," Roger admitted.

"My boy, you set a school record: four minutes, five point five seconds."

"Really?" Roger was astonished. Although he knew he was fast, he'd never timed himself and had had no idea he was capable of running *that* quickly.

"Coach Schultz told me we haven't had anyone as fast as you since some fella back in fifty-six. Of course I wasn't here at the time, so I've got to take the coach's word for it. But believe me, Roger, I liked what I saw out there." He paused, then frowned slightly. "Weren't you wearing those clothes out on the field?"

"Yes, sir," Roger said with shame. "It's all I have."

Mr. Cooper leaned over his desk to his intercom. "Rosemary," he spoke into it. "Bring me one of those sweat suits, please—in a large." Looking back at Roger, he said, "Don't you worry, my boy, we'll have you out of those things in no time."

"Really, Mr. Cooper, you don't have to—" Roger began.

"Of course I don't. It's my pleasure," Mr. Cooper said. "I don't have to tell you how important the Bart is. Big press coverage. And no one from Sweet Valley has won in years. You're our only hope, Roger. We're counting on you."

"I don't know. . . ."

"Where's your confidence, my boy? The coach tells me you didn't even practice for the race. With a little help and work, you could break four minutes at the Bart. Nobody from any of the other schools runs like that. Why, hardly anyone in the country does. Do you know what I'm talking about?"

Roger knew only too well. The Bart could be the first rung of a ladder that could lead to the state track finals, NCAAs, the AAUs—perhaps even the Olympics. *Could.* Perhaps for a boy like Bruce Patman, who had the time and money to devote to nurturing his talent. Not someone like Roger, who had to retire from racing even before he got started. What good was talent when you couldn't develop it?

Before Roger could tell Mr. Cooper that he

wouldn't be able to run, Rosemary entered the office with an official Sweet Valley High warm-up suit. Roger's eyes opened wide. He'd seen the suit many times in the school store and had always longed to have one just like it. But coming up with the thirty dollars it cost was next to impossible for him.

Mr. Cooper took it from Rosemary and handed it to Roger. "From everyone at Sweet Valley to you."

"Thank you," Roger said. "I don't know what to say."

"Just say you're going to break four minutes next Saturday afternoon. We're counting on you."

With the blue running outfit now in his hands, Roger couldn't muster up the nerve to tell Mr. Cooper he wouldn't be there. "Th-thank you," Roger said, rising from his seat. "I—I really have to get to class now."

Feeling a bit like a little boy with a new Christmas present, Roger walked out into the deserted hallway and entered the first bathroom he could find. Shedding his faded fatigues and ragged T-shirt, he tried on the new sweats. They couldn't have fit any better if they had been custom-made, and with the bright red Sweet Valley High emblem, he truly felt like a winner. He ached to savor the feeling as long as he could.

* * *

Even champions couldn't escape the mediocrity of the Sweet Valley High cafeteria food. As Roger passed through the lunch line later that morning, he halfheartedly grabbed a plate of the day's entree, beef goulash.

Jessica and Lila were already sitting at a table as he moved through the line.

"Now there's a class-A bod," Lila said, admiring the back of the lean, tall boy dressed in a blue running suit.

"You can't even see his face from here," Jessica pointed out. "But I can see even in those baggy sweats that everything's in the right place."

"Wonder who he is?" Lila asked, then gasped as he turned around and headed for the cashier. "Good grief, it's Roger!"

"So he finally traded in his ditchdigging outfit for some real clothes," Jessica added.

In his new outfit Roger fit in well with the rest of the Sweet Valley students. He didn't look different at all.

"Hey, look what I've been missing out on," Lila said admiringly. "You know, that guy *is* kind of cute when you think about it. I was only kidding around with him after the race, but you might have a point, Jess, about the value of hanging out with him for a while."

"The same guy you've been calling a nerd for months?" Jessica said with amusement.

"That was before," Lila proclaimed. "It's like Liz is always saying. I'm too quick to judge people by their appearances. I should have known that underneath those grungy clothes was a guy worth knowing." She rose from her chair.

"Hey, where are you going?" Jessica asked.

Lila winked. "Be back in a flash."

She reached Roger just as he was paying for his lunch. "Where are you going with that tray?" she asked.

Scanning the room quickly, Roger spotted Olivia sitting at a corner table in the back of the room. "Over there," he said, pointing in that general direction.

"No, you're not," Lila announced with finality. "You're coming with me."

Delighted by the prospect, Roger followed her to her table. Jessica, seeing the two of them approach, was doing all she could to suppress her astonishment at the entire chain of events. She still couldn't believe Lila was seriously interested in Roger.

But from the look of awe in Lila's eyes, it appeared she was. "I saved this seat for you," she told him, taking his tray and setting it down for him. "I'm sure you know how proud everyone is of you."

"Thank you, Lila," he said. "You realize that

if it hadn't been for you, I probably wouldn't have run today."

"I'm so glad you had the good sense to listen."

"We knew you had it in you from the way you run around campus all the time." Jessica decided to add her two cents' worth just in case Lila was playing for keeps.

"Practice makes perfect," he said weakly, reaching for the roll on his plate.

"Oooh, let me do that," Lila said, taking the pat of butter and his knife away from him.

This is getting crazier by the minute, Jessica thought. Lila must have been more desperate for a boy than she'd realized.

Just then Bruce walked by with Ken Matthews. "Say, Mr. Wonderful." Lila grabbed Bruce by his custom-tailored shirt and made him stop in his tracks. "Aren't you going to congratulate my friend over here?"

"Your friend?" Bruce said sarcastically. He didn't dare continue, though, as Lila glared at him. The girl could be dangerous if she wanted, and even Bruce lay back when he could see she meant business.

"Yes, my friend," she said. "My *dear* friend Roger, the champion of Sweet Valley. So what do you say, Bruce?"

"Congratulations, Roger." Setting down his tray on an adjacent table, he extended his hand to Roger, who shook it with pleasure. "What can I say? You ran a great race."

"So did you, Bruce."

"But don't get too cocky," Bruce added, "because now that I know you're around, I'm going to be prepared. Just keep your eyes open next week. And let that be a warning to you."

Roger wasn't about to say there wasn't going to be a next week for him, not with the adoration he could see in Lila's eyes. The hug she'd given him on the field wasn't a farce. She truly liked him.

Even if he'd been inclined to confess the truth right then, he would have been stopped by John Pfeifer, who approached the group. "Well, well, I'm in luck. I caught the two champions at once. Congratulations, guys. Roger, can I talk to you later? I want to do a special profile on you for *The Oracle*."

"I'm busy after school," Roger admitted.

"I understand. Practice and all," John answered for him. "Maybe we can talk now. What I'm really interested in is where you learned to run so well."

"I kind of fell into it. You know me," he answered lightly, "always running around campus and everything."

"But you must be doing all that running for a reason. Where do you run *to* after school, for instance?"

Roger felt himself redden. "Oh, nowhere in particular," he fibbed. "You know the old saying, run for your life? There's a history of heart disease in my family, and I want to make sure that nothing happens to me." That much was true; his mother did suffer from a heart ailment that had forced her to retire from her assembly-line job at one of the Patman factories. "Running around the way I do helps build up the cardio-vascular system."

"Aha, an athlete who knows his biology," John said admiringly.

"Well, I'd like to be a doctor someday." Roger revealed his most precious dream.

"A doctor?" Lila's opinion of Roger shot up another ten points. "What kind?"

Jessica smirked. "Does it make any difference to you, Lila?"

Lila looked at her friend as if she were a pile of dirt. "I just thought, Roger, that with your interest in the heart, you might be thinking about heart surgery or something like that."

"To tell you the truth, Lila, I haven't made up my mind," he said, not adding that at this point he would be lucky if he could put himself through college, let alone medical school. "But cardiology is certainly a strong possibility."

"I'm very impressed," Lila said.

Meanwhile, at another table, Elizabeth sat down with Enid and Todd. It was the first chance she'd had to be with her boyfriend since the race, and she was dying to know why he'd run.

Todd put down his fork as he began speaking. "It doesn't make any difference. I didn't qualify."

"Hey, that doesn't matter to me," Elizabeth said sympathetically.

"Yeah, Todd," Enid added, smiling, "we still like you."

Todd grinned. "Oh, I knew I didn't really have a shot. Yesterday Bruce got me riled up enough to want to enter the race but it wasn't until I heard about the coach this morning that I actually decided to do it. You know, just to show some support for him and the running program." He leaned back, propping his long legs up on the chair opposite his. "I'm sure going to miss the old guy."

"Miss him? Where's he going?" Elizabeth asked.

"Haven't you heard? The coach is retiring after the Bart."

"You mean the board's actually forcing him out? I didn't think they could do that."

Todd shook his head violently. "Hey, that's not it at all." He lowered his voice to a whisper. "The word is he's a very sick man."

"Where'd you hear that?" Elizabeth grew concerned.

"Neil O'Donovan told me he'd overheard the coach talking to a doctor about some tests. Neil couldn't tell for certain, but he said it seemed as if they were talking about the big C."

"Cancer." Elizabeth shuddered. "You mean he's sick enough to have to leave school?"

"Poor guy," Enid said. "And here I thought

he was just having hassles with the board. At least he has a great chance to go out a winner. Roger Barrett was fantastic."

"Yeah, you should have been on the track with him," Todd said admiringly. "I used to think I moved pretty quickly, but that guy practically broke the sound barrier."

"Well, it looks as if he's recuperating from the race in grand style," Elizabeth noted wryly, amused at the way Lila was putting her hands all over him, claiming him as her personal prize.

A few minutes before the bell rang, Roger jumped out of his seat as if he suddenly remembered something important. "Please excuse me, Lila. I've got to go."

"OK, Roger. See you at the Dairi Burger?" When he shook his head, she said, "Oh, yeah, you've got practice. I'll call you tonight, OK?"

"I'd love it," he responded.

Still carrying his empty tray, he approached Olivia, who'd chosen to avoid the crowd in favor of spending the entire lunch break in a corner huddled over her note pad. Strong emotions such as hurt and envy always brought out the best of her poetic instincts, and without even realizing it, she had managed to pour out nearly five pages in that short span of time.

Roger took a seat next to her and, as was his custom, made a move to read what she had written. But Olivia snatched up the pad and closed it before he had a chance to see a word. "Hey, why can't I see it?" he asked.

"It's not very good," she lied, unwilling to have him read her most private thoughts, the ones that concerned him and his apparent preference for Lila over her.

"Won't you let me be the judge of that?"

"I think I'm a pretty fair judge of my own work," she said with uncharacteristic bitterness.

Roger picked up on her moodiness. "Liv, what's wrong?"

She tossed back her long hair. "Nothing's wrong, Roger. Things have never been better."

Olivia had never been much of a liar, and Roger sensed a problem. "Hey, did something happen in one of your classes this morning?" he pursued.

"No," she said. "I told you everything's fine. Don't worry about me, OK?"

Roger shook his head. "No, it's not OK. You're hiding something, Liv. You seemed to be pretty upset after the race, too, and I want to know why. Are you mad at me about something?"

"Of course not!" Olivia lied. "Why in the world would I be mad at you?"

"Beats me." Roger shrugged. "I mean, I'd never intentionally do anything to hurt you."

Olivia didn't have the nerve to confess what was truly bothering her. "An apology's not necessary, Rog. I'm just in one of my silly moods. It'll pass."

"Are you sure? I hate to see you so down."

"Don't let it worry you. Really. The blues do have their advantages, believe it or not. Some of my favorite poems were written from the depths of depression. But let's not talk about me. After all, this is your special day." Olivia forced herself to smile.

"Sure is." Roger grinned, still proud of his victory. "You can't imagine how happy I am. Just think—me, the new school star! I still can't believe it. I got this new outfit. What do you think, Liv?" He held out his sweat-shirted arms for inspection.

"A little too jockish for my tastes, but I've got to say it looks great on you. Where'd you get it?"

"Can you keep a secret?" Before waiting for her answer, Roger told her, "Chrome Dome gave it to me for winning the race. He called me into his office and—"

"Roger, you're still here!" Lila's gushy voice pierced the air. Not caring that she was interrupting their conversation, she wiggled her way between Roger and Olivia. "I'm so glad I caught you," she purred. "Would you walk me to my next class?"

"I'd love to," Roger answered, forgetting about his new outfit and oblivious to the way Olivia's face fell as he turned his attention to the other girl.

Quickly Olivia rose and excused herself. "Um,

I've got to stop at the *Oracle* office before my next class. See you later," she announced.

Olivia might have slipped away without saying anything—Roger hadn't heard her anyway. In a dreamlike daze he walked out of the cafeteria arm in arm with Lila, wondering how long he could make his good fortune last.

Seven

At four-forty in the afternoon Trudy handed Jessica a small stack of documents. "Two copies of each," she barked.

Jessica had been anticipating this moment the entire day. It was the start of phase two of her plan to snag Dennis. Shortly after her arrival at work, when Trudy had been on her coffee break, Jessica had opened up the copier and turned off one of the switches. But Trudy would never know that by the totally innocent gasp that came from Jessica when she pressed the button and the machine wouldn't start.

Before Trudy had a chance to say anything, Jessica glanced behind the unit. "It's plugged in," Jessica reported. Checking the side of the machine, she added, "The paper bin's full, too. I don't understand what's wrong."

"Oh, dear," Trudy fretted. "Your father needs these papers right away. And it's too late to call for service." She looked up at the wall clock. "Jessica, I'm going to have to ask you to run down to the Copy-Rite on Main Street. I hope they're not too busy."

Jessica picked up the papers and began to leave the room. But before she'd taken more than three steps down the hall, she turned on her heel and ran back into the utility room as if struck with sudden inspiration. "Trudy, if my father needs these right away, why don't I just go across the hall and ask to use their machine? It's only a few pages. I'm sure they wouldn't mind."

"That's a wonderful idea, Jessica," Trudy said. "Good thinking."

Jessica beamed—but not for the reason Trudy thought. So far her plan was going exactly the way she had imagined, and in a few minutes she'd be seeing Dennis Creighton once again.

Fluffing her hair with her fingertips so it lay like spun gold on her shoulders, Jessica entered the reception area of the Creighton-Pawling Agency. "Dennis Creighton, please," she announced in her most businesslike voice.

"Do you have an appointment?" the receptionist asked.

"No," Jessica admitted, "but I'm sure he'll see me. Tell him Jessica Wakefield is here."

The receptionist, an older, very attractive redhead, entered the inner office, returning almost immediately. "Mr. Creighton will be right out," she said. "Have a seat, miss."

"If you don't mind, I think I'll stand," Jessica told her.

The woman shrugged. "Suit yourself."

Jessica was examining a perfume ad on the far wall when Dennis came out to greet her. "Like it?" he asked. "They're our biggest account."

Jessica turned around and smiled. He was as handsome as she'd remembered, and the conservative dress pants and shirt he wore gave him the air of sophistication Jessica liked in a boy. "It's good," she told him. "It's—it's—" Surprisingly, she found herself at a loss for words.

"Sexy?" he finished the sentence for her. "That's the message we're trying to get across."

"I'd say you've succeeded," Jessica said, referring not only to the ad. She hoped Dennis picked up her meaning.

He moved slightly closer. "Now, what can I do for you?" he asked.

If the receptionist hadn't been eyeing them, Jessica was sure he'd have touched her then. She could feel the electricity building between them. Obviously he had been doing some thinking about her in the hours since they'd last met.

Jessica looked down at the file folder in her hand. "Our copier broke down, and I was wondering—"

Dennis didn't let her finish. "Follow me," he

72

said, opening the door to the inner office. He led her down a wide hallway lined with offices on one side and framed print ads on the other, stopping when he reached a room with a sign: Copying Center—Authorized Personnel Only. Taking a key from his pocket, he opened the door. "Dad found so many of the staff using the machines for personal reasons, he was forced to put them off limits." After he led her inside, he closed the door behind them. "Pretty smart of him, don't you think?" Leaning against the machine, he looked into her eyes with undisguised desire. "There's plenty of privacy."

"It's certainly helped me out. I can do my work without having to wait in line," Jessica said, starting to feed the documents into the machine. The electricity was crackling now, and she felt the need to keep a little space between them—at least until her work was done.

Dennis picked up the finished copies. "That's not what you really came in here for, is it?" When he handed her the papers, he let his fingers linger on hers just long enough for Jessica to feel a sharp tingle of electricity. "Believe me, no one will bother us in here. It's almost quitting time."

There was no doubt the attraction was there, and if she had wanted to, Jessica could have let herself be wrapped in his arms at that very moment. But she had enough wits about her and enough concern for her father not to let his work suffer because of her. "Our office is open till six. My father really does need these copies," she told Dennis, "and I have to be getting back. . . ." She let her last few words sort of drift off as if she were leaving another thought unsaid.

"Well, what are you doing after work?"

"Oh, I don't know," she said, running her hand up his arm. "What do you have in mind?"

"How about if I meet you at your office, and we could finish this conversation." Among other things, he might well have added.

"Deal," she said. Dennis's pull on her was almost hypnotic, and it took nearly all her strength to turn around and head for the door. "I'll be waiting for you," she said, letting herself out.

Triumphantly Jessica glided into her father's office. Dennis had all the makings of a great catch, and she couldn't wait for six o'clock to arrive. She was glad she'd be meeting him at her father's office. The more she thought about it, the more the idea appealed to her. It was the perfect place for them to spend their first date. They'd have plenty of privacy—something a place like the Dairi Burger certainly couldn't offer—and that was nothing to be sniffed at, especially if Dennis's intentions were anything like her own.

Jessica quickly collated the documents, then

entered her father's office. "Copied and collated, Mr. Wakefield," she said with authority.

"Thank you, Jessica," he said, his fatherly pride showing through as he stuffed the papers into his attaché case. "Now I'll be able to make the meeting on time."

"I'm here to do anything I can to help," she said. "But before you go, I have a favor I'd like to ask you. I've got a ton of homework that's due tomorrow, and it'd really help me out if I could stay here for a while and work on it."

"Why can't you do it at home?"

"Oh, Daddy, you know my friends. The phone at home will probably be ringing all night. Here I know I'll have the peace and quiet I need."

"OK, Jess," her father said. "But only on two conditions. One, you don't stay later than nine o'clock, and two, that you ring up the night guard and have him escort you to the car. You can't be too safe around here at night."

"Sure thing, Daddy." She gave him a kiss. "Have a good meeting."

"See you at home," her father said. "I can't tell you, Jess, how happy it makes me to see you becoming so responsible. Just don't work yourself too hard now."

"Don't worry, Daddy, I won't," she assured him. Far from it. If her plan continued to go as she'd envisioned it, she was in for one of the most pleasurable evenings she'd had in a long time.

Jessica arrived home that night at nine-thirty. When Elizabeth came into Jessica's room to find out whether or not her sister was enjoying the working world, she was puzzled by the look of rapture on her twin's face. "I can't believe how two days of work have changed you, Jess. Dad said you actually stayed late to do homework?"

Her twin picked up a nail file from her night table and began working on her nails. In a hushed voice she said, "Please don't tell Dad, but that's not why I stayed. I don't want to get into this with him, Liz, but his office is a mess. Supplies are all over the place, and there doesn't seem to be an orderly system of doing anything."

Elizabeth was perplexed. "That doesn't sound like Dad, Jess."

"Liz, you haven't been in his office since that witch Trudy arrived." She said the name as if it were a plague. "She's awful. I don't know why Dad keeps her on. Anyway, I spent the entire time straightening out the supply room. It'll probably take me a couple of days to finish working it all out. Don't tell Dad, though. I want it to be a surprise."

Elizabeth lowered herself onto a corner of Jessica's unmade bed. "I have to admit I would never have thought you'd take to work the way you have."

"I'm really committed to it," Jessica said, her

mind on the delectable way Dennis's kisses set her neck on fire. Phase two had been a stunning success, even better than she'd planned. "Putting in a few extra hours is the least I can do. Besides, I do have an ulterior motive."

Elizabeth cut in. "I knew there was something else going on. Dad get a new office boy?"

"Elizabeth Wakefield, you've got a one-track mind!" Jessica said petulantly, crossing her legs underneath her as she began to file the nails on her other hand. "I wasn't even thinking about boys," she lied. "What I was *going* to say—before you so rudely interrupted me—is that I'd like to be doing more than office chores. I'm hoping that Dad will see my interest and make me his assistant. You may not believe it, Liz, but for the first time in my life I'm actually anxious to go to work." She put down her file. "I don't even miss going to the Dairi Burger."

"It's only been two days," Elizabeth pointed out.

"Two of the most rewarding days of my life." Jessica got up and pranced toward her desk. "Now, if you'll excuse me, I'm going to have to ask you to leave. I really do have some homework for tomorrow, and if it's going to get done, I have to start now." She flung open her French book and began to read it even before Elizabeth left the room.

But Jessica couldn't concentrate on the assignment—not that she had really expected to be able to. She just wanted some privacy to replay the evening with Dennis in her mind. It hadn't taken them long to dispense with the formalities and take up where they'd left off in Dennis's father's office. His kisses were as satisfying as Jessica could want, and he was eager to please her, though enough of a gentleman to realize when their passions were reaching the point beyond which they would no longer be able to control themselves.

Dennis didn't seem to mind at all when Jessica had suggested spending the entire date in the office. In fact, it was his idea they meet there again the following evening. That suited Jessica's plans for phase three perfectly. The way she figured it, by the end of the week he'd be hooked on her for sure and more than willing to pick her up at her house for a regular date. Then she'd feel justified in quitting her job, which she found to be nothing but drudgery. A week was long enough to serve as a trial period for anyone, and even Elizabeth would be convinced that her attempt at working had been a sincere one. Everybody would be happy, Jessica concluded, looking forward to the day she could stop keeping Dennis a secret and introduce him to the rest of the world.

Two days later, Lila, Jessica, and Cara were standing in line at the cafeteria. Lila seemed preoccupied, searching the room furtively with her deep brown eyes and hoping Jessica wouldn't notice.

But she should have known better than to think she could keep anything from Jessica. Even though it was twin sister Elizabeth who wrote the school's gossip column, Jessica was a master snoop and always made it her business to know everything that was going on. "Who are you looking for?" she asked Lila as they approached the counter.

"Oh, no one in particular," Lila said breezily.

Jessica lowered an eyebrow. "Could it be Roger, perhaps?"

Lila sighed. "For a guy who's had a crush on me for months, he sure is playing hard to get." Lila paid for her lunch and joined Jessica and Cara at a table on the patio. "I decided to watch him practice yesterday, but he never showed up. When I finally got him on the phone last night, he said some family thing had come up, something he didn't want to talk about. I asked him to join me here for lunch today, and he said he was flattered, but now I'm not so sure he's going to show up."

"That's surprising, considering the way he'd been salivating after you like a hungry puppy." Jessica took a large bite out of her cheeseburger.

Lila looked at her friend with envy. She couldn't see how Jessica could eat so much and never gain an ounce. Lila had to work like crazy to keep her slender figure. "I wonder where he could be?"

"Maybe he has to practice," Cara pointed out. "The coach might have him making up yesterday's session."

"You're a genius, Cara. That's got to be it," Lila agreed. "We really did have a wonderful talk last night. He's actually a funny guy. Did you know he does an absolutely wicked imitation of Mademoiselle Dalton?"

"I'm sure that made him score a lot of points in your book," Jessica noted. The young French teacher had dated Lila's father for a while, and she and Lila were hardly what anyone would call best buddies.

"And did you notice the way everyone is talking about him? Overnight he's become the darling of the entire school."

"And now you intend to make him your darling, right?" Cara asked.

Lila took a sip of her soda. "You'd better believe it, honey."

"Has he asked you out yet?" Jessica asked.

"No. I get the feeling Roger's a little shy around girls. But don't think that's going to stop me. I have my ways. You just wait and see who'll be with Roger at the Bart dance."

Roger had just finished taking a quiz in his Spanish class the following Monday afternoon when he was called down to Coach Schultz's office. He took his time walking down the empty hallway, fully aware of the reason he was being summoned.

He dreaded the confrontation, realizing he should have cleared up this matter the week before. But the temptation to hold onto his newfound status was too overwhelming to resist. Every morning as he dressed for school he'd tell himself this was the day he'd tell the coach the truth. But then he'd run into someone on the lush Sweet Valley campus who would give him the thumbs-up sign or tell him how the school was rooting for him, and his resolve would crumble. The people watching him held looks of admiration and respect, things he'd never before experienced and probably never would again once he announced his intention not to run.

Coach Schultz was leaning back in his old wooden swivel chair when Roger arrived. He was grim-faced as usual, but Roger could detect a further hardening in the coach's expression as he walked into the office. "Take a seat, Roger," he said.

The boy sat in the only seat available, a wooden stool to the right of the desk. His knees buckled under his jeans.

The coach got right to the point. "What kind of game are you trying to play?" he asked. "When I order you to practice, I expect you to be there. You think you're so special you don't need it?"

"No, sir," Roger interjected. "That's not it."

The coach went on. "Now take Patman. I expected him to be the cocky one, giving me a lot of sass about running extra laps and wind sprints. But no, he shows up after school—much to my surprise, I might say—ready for practice. You put a scare into him, my boy. He doesn't like to lose, and he's going all out to win. Which is more than I can say for you."

"I know what you're thinking," Roger began. "And I can explain—"

"You have no idea what I'm thinking, son." The coach rose and turned around to the bulletin board behind his desk. "You see this fella?" he asked, pointing to a faded black-and-white photo. "That's Jack Ralston. Do you know what he's doing today?"

Roger shook his head. "No, sir."

"He's the president of one of the largest research labs in the state," he said with obvious pride. "And to a large degree he owes it all to the Bart. That's what I'm thinking about, Roger. I'm thinking about what the Bart can do for you and how you appear to be letting it slip through your fingers."

"I'm not following you, sir."

"I'm talking about the scholarship. Jack couldn't afford to go to college until the Bart came along. The scholarship he won to Sweet

Valley College gave him an education he might never have received. You want to go on to college, don't you, Roger?"

"Yes, Coach."

"A full scholarship to Sweet Valley College could make all the difference in the world. Why are you throwing away your chance?" Coach Schultz said, the anger evident in his voice. "You're a fine runner, and my money's on you to win, but you don't stand a ghost of a chance if you don't practice." The coach paused as the bell rang. "Think about it, Roger. I want to see you at practice this afternoon. I've got to get to the gym now."

Coach Schultz picked up his whistle and walked out of the room, leaving Roger to think over what he had said. Roger knew the coach was right, but even the grand prize of a full scholarship would be useless if he lost his job. The way Roger figured it, with his good grades he stood an excellent chance of winning a scholarship anyway. But he needed the money from his job right now to help pay his family's bills. And winning the race wasn't a sure thing, anyway. If he took the chance of losing his job and ended up losing the race, too, he'd wind up with nothing. By not running in the race, at least he wouldn't be any worse off than he was now.

Roger was preoccupied with his situation as he walked down the hallway to his next class.

He didn't even notice Lila approaching until they practically bumped into each other.

"Well, well, if this isn't a pleasant surprise," Lila said, smiling sweetly.

"Oh, hi, Lila," Roger said, a smile lighting up his own face. "Sorry I couldn't join you at lunch today. I had to practice." Actually he'd been doing his homework in the library.

"Oh, that's OK," Lila said. "But I'm glad I caught you. How'd your practice go?"

Roger shuffled his feet uneasily. "Oh, well, OK," he lied.

Lila smiled. "Don't be so modest. You're very talented, and there's nothing wrong with letting the world know about it. In fact, I even wrote a little poem about you. I wanted to have it run in *The Oracle*, but your *friend* Olivia rejected it. I'd like you to hear it, though. Got a second?"

Roger was amazed that Lila had taken the time to write about him. "Sure, go ahead."

Lila deftly plucked a folded piece of white paper from her shoulder bag and began to read dramatically.

Roger Barrett, a boy so fine.
His speedy running is so divine.
In school, too, he is very smart.
He'll walk away with the trophy at the Bart.
In everything he operates at the highest stratum.
We at Sweet Valley are so proud we have him.

*   *   *

She paused to let the words sink in. "Well, what do you think?"

"Um, what can I say? Thanks." Roger was glad Olivia had had the good sense to save Lila the humiliation of having it published. The poem was awful. "It was very thoughtful of you," he added diplomatically.

"I know," Lila said. "I just wanted to make sure you realize that we're all behind you one hundred percent. We want you to win. I've even asked Jessica to write a new cheer for you for the race." Lila clapped her hand to her mouth. "I don't believe I said that. It was supposed to be a surprise."

"You shouldn't have gone to all that trouble, Lila. Really you shouldn't have," Roger emphasized.

"There's that modesty again." Lila shook her head. "It's my *pleasure* to do these things for you. I was also thinking you're probably going to be very hot and tired after your race practice today. Why don't you join me for a little swim in my pool?"

Roger's eyes grew wide. He couldn't imagine anything he'd like more—and anything that was so far from ever becoming a reality. "I'd like to," he said. "But I can't."

"Why not?" Lila pouted, fingering his shirt seductively. "What can you be doing that's more important than that?"

"I—I can't tell you," he said. "Not yet. Listen, I've got to get to class. I'll talk to you later." He ran down the hall before Lila had the chance to make him say something he knew he shouldn't.

"We'll see what happens," Lila said, her face hardening. She wasn't used to being turned down, and she didn't like it.

Eight

Elizabeth Wakefield peered around the stairwell door in her father's office building and looked down the hallway. She felt a little silly playing detective, but she'd come to the conclusion that she'd never figure out what her sister was doing unless she saw it herself. For an entire week Jessica had been staying late at the office, but her reasoning was starting to wear a little thin. How long could it take to fix up a supply cabinet?

When she had entered the building, Elizabeth had had to sign in at the night guard's desk. She had deliberately scrawled her name illegibly—she didn't want anyone to recognize it. She was glad she had worn her jacket with a hood; with her hair covered and the hood tied closely around her face, the guard would be less likely to mistake her for Jessica. As she was about to get on the elevator, she had spotted Roger Barrett making his way toward the front of the building, pulling his mop and pail along-side him. Not wanting to embarrass him and not wanting to be spotted herself, Elizabeth had slunk toward the stairs and quietly walked up the four flights to her father's floor.

Now, she tiptoed toward the office. Through the frosted glass door, she could see the silhouettes of two people standing close together, and from the sound of things, it appeared they weren't talking about legal matters.

"Mmm . . ." Jessica murmured. "No one kisses the way you do."

"There's plenty more where that came from," Dennis said.

So it *was* a boy, Elizabeth thought, her deepest suspicions confirmed.

"How'd you like that?" Dennis asked softly after what must have been one of the longest kisses in Sweet Valley history.

"Delicious," Jessica said, snuggling up to him. "But doesn't it bother you just a teensy bit that we spend all our time in this office?"

"I'd hardly call this suffering. Would you?"

"Well, no . . ." Jessica began.

Dennis continued. "Besides, where else can we go? Your dad thinks you're here doing your homework. What if he were to call up and get no answer?"

"I'm not necessarily talking about weeknights," Jessica hinted.

"We're just getting to know each other. We've

got plenty of time," Dennis told her. "There's no need to rush into anything."

Jessica sighed. "I suppose you're right." It wasn't her style to give up so easily, but she didn't want to let Dennis think she cared that much.

The blond-haired boy traced Jessica's lips with his fingertip. "Hey, no frowns allowed here." He kissed her once gently, then again, with more insistence. "Tell you what. Let's go out right now."

"But what about Dad?"

Dennis thought a moment. "Call him up and tell him you're going to grab a bite to eat before coming home."

"Great thinking," Jessica said, brightening considerably. She got up and went to the phone.

That was Elizabeth's signal to make herself invisible. Moving like a cheetah, she found refuge behind a nearby water fountain and waited for them to come out of the office.

The boy was helping Jessica on with her sweater. "What do you say we go to Guido's? It's close by, and then afterward I'll walk you to your car," he said, leading her toward the elevator.

Normally Jessica left before Dennis and had the night guard see her to her car. "Oh, I was hoping you'd give me a ride home, Dennis. I didn't bring my car today. My sister begged me to lend it to her, and I couldn't bear to turn her down."

Elizabeth resented being used as a convenient excuse for her twin. The only reason she herself had the car that night was because their mother had needed it during the day and had turned down Jessica's request for it. The twins were allowed to use the little red Fiat only when their mother didn't need it for her job as an interior designer. Elizabeth knew their parents would be furious if they discovered the real reason Jessica had been begging them to lend her the car the previous week. Jessica had convinced them that the buses ran so infrequently that she needed the car if she was going to stay late at the office to do her homework. Fortunately for Jessica, Alice Wakefield's design business was going through a slow period, so she hadn't needed the car as much as usual, and she had been very pleased that her normally flighty daughter was becoming so serious and responsible.

Dennis, of course, was unaware of Jessica's lies as he brushed his lips against her forehead. "What timing," he declared. "I'm having a lot of trouble with my car, and it's in the shop. I've got to take the bus home. Sorry, Jess."

She didn't seem to mind. "That's OK. We'll wait at the bus stop together then," she said as the elevator arrived.

The imitation wood elevator doors opened,

and Roger Barrett, dressed in his institutional green janitorial uniform, stepped out with his bucket and mop. A shock of recognition registered on his face and on Jessica's, but neither one said anything as their paths crossed. Elizabeth felt her stomach churn in pity for the boy. By tomorrow morning his secret would be common knowledge around school, and once again he'd be the laughingstock of Sweet Valley.

Unless Elizabeth acted—and acted quickly. Sneaking back down the stairs, she waited until Jessica and Dennis had signed out. Then she, too, signed out and hurried down the street in the opposite direction from Jessica and Dennis. Jumping into the Fiat, which she had parked on a side street, she quickly put the key in the ignition. She wanted to be home well before Jessica.

Roger knew he was in trouble. He needed some advice, and as soon as he got home that evening, he reached for the phone and dialed Olivia's number.

"I've got problems, Liv," he confessed to her.

Olivia was surprised to hear Roger's voice. She'd gone out of her way to avoid him ever since he'd won the race trials and, apparently, Lila Fowler's heart as well. The sight of the two of them together was a painful reminder of how much she was missing out on and how much she truly cared for Roger.

"What's wrong?" she asked, concerned.

"First off, there's something I've got to explain to you. You know how I've told you I spend most of my time studying? I lied, Liv. My family's a lot poorer than I've led you to believe, and I've got to work to help pay the rent. Every day after school I'm a janitor in an office building."

For a few seconds the line was quiet as Olivia absorbed the news.

"Go on, say it," Roger continued. "It embarrasses you to realize you're friends with a cleaning boy. If you don't want to be my friend anymore, I'll understand, so just—"

"Roger Barrett, that's the most ridiculous thing I've ever heard," Olivia cut him off. "I don't find anything wrong with your being a janitor—except that I wish you'd told me sooner. I have a feeling *you're* the one who's ashamed. You have no reason to be, you realize."

"Oh, no? It's bad enough I've had to spend my life having people laugh behind my back about my clothes. The last thing I need is for the whole school to find out I clean other people's bathrooms."

"So what if they know? The people who find something funny about that aren't your friends and they never will be. But there are plenty of kids out there who'd admire you for what you're doing."

Roger sighed. "Well, it looks as if I'm about to find out if you're right."

"*I* don't plan on telling anyone, if that's what you mean," Olivia said.

"Oh, I know you wouldn't. It's Jessica Wakefield I'm concerned about. I ran into her tonight at the office building. I'm sure she's on the phone with her friends already."

"Even if she tells the world, I don't see that you have anything to worry about. You're a big star in school, Roger. The fact that you're helping out your family can only make you a bigger hero."

"Well, that's the other thing I'm calling about. The star is about to fall. I can't run in the Bart. I don't have the guts to tell anyone. You're the only person who knows."

"Why can't you run?"

"My boss, Mr. Pendergast, is a real rat. I know he won't give me the time off on Saturday to race, let alone some time to practice during the week."

"Have you asked him?"

"I'm afraid to, Liv. A few weeks ago I asked him for an afternoon off so I could take my mother to the clinic. He gave me an hour off— and even *that* was like pulling teeth—but then he warned me that if I asked him for any more time off, he'd consider it my resignation notice."

"He can't do that!" Olivia declared.

"He's the boss," Roger pointed out. "He never loses an opportunity to let me know how lucky I am to have the job. I can be replaced very easily."

"I doubt that, Roger. But in any event, there's got to be a way to get you to run. Now it's clearer than ever that you really could use that scholarship—certainly a lot more than Bruce Patman could. Tell you what. Let me think about it and see what I can come up with."

"Thanks, Liv. You're a good friend."

For a long time after she got off the phone with Roger, Olivia pondered the situation. Lila or no Lila, her feelings for Roger were as strong as ever. It killed her that the only thing keeping him from a possible college education was a mean-spirited boss. She'd had enough run-ins with her superiors at the museum to know the kind of pressure he faced. Try as she did, however, she couldn't figure out a way to help him. That's why she decided to betray his confidence and call up someone who might.

On the other side of town, in a corner bedroom of the Fowler mansion, Lila looked out her window and gazed at the twinkling lights of the Sweet Valley houses below. She was racking her brain trying to figure out what she was doing wrong. Beyond a shadow of a doubt, she knew Roger had a crush on her, yet he still hadn't asked her to the Bart dance. So far he'd been resisting all her hints; he'd even turned down an invitation from her. True, her interest in him had been rather sudden, given the way she used to ignore him. But all that was in the past. Everyone had misjudged Roger, and now that he'd won the race and proved he was one of them, things were going to be different. Together she and Roger would be the new golden couple in school, even more popular than the short-lived though spectacular team of Jessica Wakefield and Bruce Patman.

There had to be some way she could ensure that she would be the one on Roger's arm at the dance. But all her efforts had failed, and she had run out of fresh ideas. So she did the only thing left to do. Grabbing the phone off her night table, she quickly dialed a number, tapping one perfectly manicured, frosted fingernail against the receiver as she waited impatiently for an answer.

"Jessica?" she said. "I need your help."

The girl on the other end cut her off. "Lila, it's Liz. Jessica isn't home yet." Thank goodness, Elizabeth wanted to add. Lila Fowler was the last person in the world her sister ought to be talking to at the moment.

"Don't tell me she's working late again."

"Afraid so," Elizabeth said, figuring Lila didn't

need to hear the truth from her. "She's very committed to this job."

"I think your sister ought to be committed, period," Lila said huffily. "If she keeps this up, she's not going to have any friends left. What good is having a friend who's not around when you really need her?"

"Jessica hasn't forgotten you, Lila. She should be home soon, and I'll tell her you called. But don't be surprised if you don't hear from her till tomorrow. I have to have a talk with her, too."

"Oh, really? What has she done to you this time, Liz?"

"Nothing," Elizabeth said pointedly. "It's only some family stuff I have to discuss with her." Just then the Wakefields' front door slammed shut. "I've got to go, Lila. See you in school tomorrow."

Elizabeth went downstairs and followed Jessica to their spacious kitchen. She watched from the doorway as Jessica took a glass from one of the cabinets and poured herself some milk. "Have a good time at work tonight?" Elizabeth asked.

Jessica nearly spilled the contents of the milk carton onto the counter. "Elizabeth, you scared me," she gasped. "I didn't know you were standing there." Recovering quickly, however, she leaned against the counter and answered her sister's question. "I had a marvelous time. I hardly even consider it work anymore."

Looking closely at her twin, Elizabeth now realized that the slightly glazed look in Jessica's eyes that she had previously attributed to fatigue after a long day was actually infatuation with this new boy. It was surprising, Elizabeth thought, that she hadn't noticed sooner. She'd certainly seen this expression on Jessica's face enough times to know what it meant. "That stands to reason, Jess. Boys do have a way of making time fly. By the way, what's his name?"

Jessica fidgeted with her glass. "I don't know what you're talking about. I've spent the past six hours in Dad's office."

"Oh, I don't doubt that," Elizabeth said. "But I know you weren't there alone."

Jessica continued her charade. "You must be imagining things, Liz."

Elizabeth walked over to the counter and said in a hushed voice, "You can cut the act, Jess. I know all about the boy. And quite honestly I'm a little hurt you haven't told me about him. From what I could see, you two make a lovely couple."

It took all the restraint Jessica could muster not to pour the rest of her milk over her sister's head. "You were spying on me!" she shouted.

Elizabeth put her finger to her lips. "Shh, Mom and Dad might hear." Using the authority that came with having a four-minute head start on life, she ordered, "Finish up your milk and come upstairs with me."

Jessica obeyed and moments later followed her twin up the staircase to her bedroom, slamming the door behind her. Now that they were alone, she felt no compulsion to take the invasion of her privacy lying down. "How could you do it?" she cried. "I can't believe my own sister has so little faith in me she feels the need to check up on my whereabouts."

"That's a funny thing to say considering my suspicions were right, Jess. But I'm not going to get into that right now. I want to talk about Roger Barrett. I know you saw him tonight, and I have to make sure you don't breathe a word to anyone."

Jessica snickered. "Why shouldn't I? It's only the hottest item to hit school in months. Big track star poses as night janitor. I suppose you want it to remain a big secret until *you* reveal it in 'Eyes and Ears'?"

"If I wanted to put it in the column, I could have done it weeks ago," Elizabeth said. "But I'm respecting Roger's wishes and keeping it confidential. The money he makes doesn't go for a car or fancy clothes or money to spend on girls—it pays his family's rent. It would kill him if anyone found out about it—and I mean *anyone*, Jessica. Understand?"

Jessica shifted her weight on Elizabeth's bed. "It'd put a big fat crimp in his relationship with Lila if she knew," Jessica said aloud. "God, I'd love to see her face when she finds out she's been chasing after a cleaning boy.''

''You're not going to tell her, are you, Jess?'' Elizabeth shook her head in exasperation. Nothing was ever easy with her sister.

''Oh, you never know,'' Jessica replied airily. ''Something that juicy might slip out accidentally.''

''Then you leave me no choice. I'll have to tell Dad what I saw tonight.'' Elizabeth sighed sadly. ''It's going to break his heart. . . .''

How can she do this? Jessica thought frantically. *She's using one of my very own tricks to get me!* It was unlike Elizabeth to resort to blackmail, but nevertheless Jessica couldn't help but feel a reluctant sense of admiration for her twin's scheme. Under the circumstances, it was in Jessica's best interest to go along with her sister's request. ''OK, you win, Liz. I'll keep my mouth shut about Roger.'' *For the time being*, she added silently, crossing her fingers behind her back.

Elizabeth gave her sister a hug. ''Thanks,'' she said. ''It really means a lot to me.''

Jessica pushed any guilt she might have felt about deceiving Elizabeth to the back of her mind. Ordinarily she'd never break a promise to her sister, but news like this was too good to be kept under wraps forever. She'd just have to be extra careful about how and when she revealed it.

''Hey,'' Jessica said, steering the subject away

from herself, "how does Todd feel about your sudden interest in Roger?" She winked. "You sure you two don't have something going on between you?" She gave Elizabeth a playful tap on the arm.

"No way," Elizabeth said. "I just feel for the guy, that's all. And now that this is settled, tell me about this guy you've been seeing."

"So you'll have more ammunition for Dad?"

"You know me better than that, Jess." Elizabeth pretended to pout. "Truthfully, I think he's cute."

Jessica smiled, glad she could at last pour out her feelings to her sister. "His name's Dennis Creighton, and his father has the office across from Daddy's. He's very nice, Liz, and very sensitive about the things that really count with a girl. I've been waiting for a guy like him to come around for a long time."

"He sounds very special to you."

"He could be," Jessica said hopefully. "Of course, given my working situation, I've only been able to spend time with him at Dad's office."

"You've got the weekends," Elizabeth pointed out.

"I know, but that's the funny thing. So far he hasn't asked me to go out with him—on a real date, that is. I'd thought by now he'd want to do other things than hang out in Daddy's office with me, but he seems content to leave it the way it is." She left unsaid her realization that until Dennis grew tired of the arrangements, she'd have to stay on a job she was hating more and more with each passing day. "Naturally, I expect to go to the Bart dance with him. But he'd better act soon. I'm a very impatient person."

"Don't I know—"

Elizabeth's response was cut short by the ring of the telephone. The twins' parents recently had had extensions installed in each of the girls' bedrooms. Jessica leaned across the bed and picked up the phone. "Oh, hi, Lila," she said cheerfully. "Hold on a sec, OK?" Holding her palm over the mouthpiece she whispered, "I'm going to take the call in my room. And don't worry about a thing." She gave Elizabeth a reassuring squeeze as she got up, then hurried through the bathroom that connected her room to her sister's.

She settled down on her own bed. "Hang up, Liz," she yelled. Then she spoke into the phone. "What's up, Lila?" she asked.

"It's about Roger," Lila said. "I've got to find a way to land him for good. I need some help. Got any ideas?"

Jessica sat straight up. It wasn't often that Lila came running to her for help. "Let me think," she said, delighted to play the role of Lila's savior. Jessica picked up her brush and began to run it through her hair. "By the way, did Roger enjoy your pool this afternoon?"

"He never made it over," Lila said. "That's part of the reason for this call. Roger's still playing hard-to-get with me. You know I usually like to take care of these things myself, but I've tried everything I can think of."

Jessica chuckled to herself. Lila sounded so desperate! "Are you sure you really want him?"

"Of course I do." Lila's patience was wearing thin. "Can't you think of anything I can do?"

"I'm not a computer, Lila. Give me some time to mull it over. I'll call you later tonight. OK?"

Jessica put down the receiver. If Lila wanted Roger, Jessica thought, she'd help her get him, even though she realized her friend would run away from Roger as fast as she could if she knew the truth about him. As open as Lila tried to appear, Jessica knew that she'd never in a million years want anything to do with him if she knew he was a poverty-stricken janitor. Lila had often commented pityingly on the boys who worked weekends at the Dairi Burger or the Valley Cinema. She couldn't see how any girl could put up with a boy who had to work Friday and Saturday nights. "What kind of relationship could someone like that ever have?" she'd often asked.

But Jessica had promised Elizabeth not to tell Lila anything, so what could she do, she thought gleefully, but come up with a way to get Lila and Roger together.

Rejecting about a dozen schemes before feeling satisfied, she finally came up with a plan she felt was destined to succeed. She snapped her fingers assuredly. Not only had she figured out a way to lure Roger to Lila's place, but she had also managed to work in a little dividend of her own. If things worked out right, she would end up the star of the party with her new boyfriend, Dennis.

Feeling proud of herself, Jessica quickly dialed Lila's number. "The wizard strikes again," she announced. "Lila, your worries are over."

"You've got a plan?"

"Do I ever. Here goes," Jessica said. "You know that Coach Schultz is leaving school after the race."

"Tom McKay told me it's because he's got cancer."

"I heard it was his heart. But that doesn't really matter. The point is he'll be gone, and the school doesn't appear to be doing a thing for him. That's where you come in. You could throw a party in his honor right before the dance Saturday night. A small affair by the pool."

"And invite Roger as my escort?" Lila filled in.

"You've got it. He may be reluctant to accept a regular invitation from you, but he can't pass up a celebration for his own coach. It'd be unethical. Then, of course, since we'll all be going to the dance from there. . . ."

"It'll be very convenient for the two of us to go together. Very clever, Jessica."

Very clever, indeed, Jessica thought, proud of coming up with a solution that dovetailed very nicely with her own desires. Dennis still hadn't asked her to the Bart dance, but she was sure he would say yes if she asked him to this party. Lila's would be the perfect place to introduce him to her friends. With so many people expected at the Bart dance, her grand arrival with Dennis might go unnoticed. But everybody who mattered could be invited to Lila's to get a first-hand look at her latest conquest.

"Talk up this party with the gang, Lila. But make sure everyone realizes it's a tribute to the coach. I just have a feeling that's the key to convincing Roger to come."

"I think it just might work, Jess," Lila said.

"I think so, too," Jessica said. But her thoughts were already focused on how she could make the most of the moment with Dennis. True, it would be Lila's party, and the attention would be centered on Lila and Roger, but Jessica had a way of fixing that, too. She could see it now. Everyone who was anyone—from her sorority sisters to the guys on the boys' tennis team— would be gathered around Lila's lushly landscaped swimming pool. Right in the center of things would be Lila, making sure everyone was aware that Roger was the object of her affection. Then, as the hors d'oeuvres were being passed around, Jessica could casually mention to Cara how nice it was that Roger got time off from cleaning toilets to come to this affair. Within minutes everyone would be looking at Lila strangely and she'd try to discover why. Soon she'd be off hiding in embarrassment, trying to figure out how to get out of this one. That would set the stage for Jessica's introduction of Dennis and her taking over as star of the party. Jessica giggled inwardly in anticipation of the event. "I'll start making calls now if you want," Jessica offered.

"Oh, that'd be terrific," Lila gushed. "I don't know what I'd do without a friend like you."

Jessica hung up then, and before she had a chance to make any calls, the phone rang again. She picked it up the same time as Elizabeth did, but when she discovered the call was not for her, Jessica hung up.

After Elizabeth got off the phone, Jessica walked into her sister's room. "Liz, has the gossip column gone to press yet?" she asked, an innocent lilt to her voice.

"I still have a couple of days. Why? Do you have something for me?"

"Only the biggest news of the year. Lila's going to have a tribute to Coach Schultz right before the dance on Saturday. All the best people will be there. It should be the party to end all parties."

From the smirk on her sister's face, Elizabeth could tell that Jessica was up to no good. "Thanks for telling me, but why should I rush it into this week's column? Parties usually make news after they've happened, not before."

"This is different," Jessica insisted. "This party is exactly what I need. It's the perfect place for me to introduce Dennis to everyone."

"Hmm, and I'll bet it's the perfect setting for Roger and Lila, too. I imagine you can't wait to see them together at the party," Elizabeth noted dryly. "But I wouldn't count on it. My hunch is that it'll never come off."

"It has to," Jessica said. "Roger might make an excuse to her about a regular party, but he can't pass this up. Look how disappointed in him the coach would be."

"I think the coach is going to be even more disappointed than you think. Because I don't think Roger's going to run in the race at all."

Jessica's jaw dropped. "You know this for a fact?"

"I was just on the phone with Olivia Davidson. She said Roger told her his boss won't give him the time off. So you can forget about your plan, Jess. It's not going to happen."

"Don't you think there's any chance you could be wrong, Liz?"

"Why? So you could get a laugh out of seeing

Lila and Roger together? Olivia said Roger's really worried you'll tell the whole school you saw him."

Jessica bypassed the issue. "My big concern is getting the chance to introduce Dennis. If Roger doesn't run, Lila won't have the party, and it'll ruin everything. Liz, isn't there something we can do? Roger's got to be in the race!"

Elizabeth stifled a giggle. She agreed with Jessica, even if her twin's motives were less than honorable. Roger's running would be a boon to Sweet Valley, and more people than the coach and Jessica and Lila would be disappointed if he failed to show up. "I want to see him run, too," Elizabeth said. "And maybe there's a way to make it happen." Struck with a thought, she got out of her desk chair and headed out to the hallway.

"Where are you going?" Jessica asked.

"I've got a brainstorm," Elizabeth said. "And if it works, you'll see Roger on the starting line—and at Lila's party—on Saturday."

Nine

The following morning Elizabeth was standing by her locker talking with Enid when Roger came whizzing down the corridor. "Roger, stop! I've got to talk to you," she called.

Roger was nearly up at the next bank of lockers when he turned around. "What's up?"

"Enid, could you excuse us a moment?" Her friend backed off gracefully as Elizabeth led Roger toward an unoccupied stretch of hallway. "I know Jessica saw you last night. I wanted to let you know that I spoke to her and she's promised not to say a word about you."

"Can you trust her?" Roger asked.

"She's my sister," Elizabeth said. "When she gives her word to me, she means it."

Roger shook his head. "I'm glad to hear that, Liz. And I appreciate what you've done for me. But I think Lila's going to find out today anyway. As soon as I can, I'm going to go to Coach

Schultz and tell him I'm dropping out of the race. The truth is I never wanted to run in the first place. It was just an ego thing for me, to see if I could do it. Well, I proved I can, and that's good enough for me. If it's not good enough for anyone else around here, that's tough."

"You don't really mean that, Roger," Elizabeth said.

"Hey, don't put words in my mouth," he said, his voice rising in anger. "This school doesn't need me, anyway. You've got Bruce Patman. That should be enough for anyone."

Elizabeth kept her voice low. "I wasn't trying to put words in your mouth," she explained. "What I meant to say was that I know you're afraid of losing your job."

"Olivia tell you?"

Elizabeth nodded. "But I think there's a way you can run and keep your job at the same time."

Roger looked at her as if she'd lost her mind. "Sure, and Santa Claus really comes down the chimney at Christmas. Maybe miracles happen in your life, Liz, but not in mine. The fantasy is over for me. At least the part about the race."

As Roger walked off, his eyes downcast, Elizabeth made a move to go after him but then changed her mind. Maybe she shouldn't tell him her father was going to plead his case with Mr. Pendergast. It was better not to offer him false hope, just in case things didn't work out.

Before heading to Coach Schultz's office, Roger went to his locker and took out and carefully folded the sweat suit the principal had given him. He didn't feel right keeping it any longer, and he planned to return it to Mr. Cooper after his meeting with the coach.

Roger should have had plenty of time to take care of everything before his first class, but he hadn't counted on running into Lila. She looked particularly attractive that day in a pale, close-fitting linen dress cut low in the back.

"Roger, I'm so glad I caught you. I have the most marvelous news to tell you."

"I have something to tell you, too," he said. His nervousness clearly apparent, he let the sweat suit topple to the floor.

Lila picked it up. "What are you carrying that around for?" she queried.

He took a deep breath. "I'm returning the suit."

"Why? Don't you like the fit? I thought it looked great on you."

"The fit has nothing to do with it. I didn't buy this suit, Lila. The principal gave it to me, a sort of thanks for winning the trials the other day."

"So why are you giving it back?"

"Lila"—he looked into her brown eyes, trying to read her thoughts—"how important is it to you that I run in the Bart?"

110

"What a silly question, Roger."

"Is it? Would your feelings about me change if I didn't run in the race?"

Lila snorted. "I'm not going to answer that, Roger, because I can't think of a single reason why you wouldn't run. It's only the most prestigious sporting event of the year."

Roger was beginning to feel sick inside. He had the awful feeling that Lila had already given him the answer he didn't want to hear, but he had to continue. She'd know soon enough, anyway.

"Well, I have a very good reason for not running," he told her. "I work in an office building, Lila. Every day from three to nine and all day Saturday you'll find me there, making sure that all the wastepaper baskets are emptied and all the floors are shining."

Lila couldn't hide the feeling of disgust that began to run through her. "You're a cleaning boy!"

"I prefer the term janitor," he said, an unexpected feeling of pride coming over him. "We're not all born rich. I don't like being poor any more than you'd like it. That's why I'm working my fingers off at this job. All that talk about wanting to be a doctor is true, Lila. I want that more than anything, and one way or another I'm going to make it. If it takes missing the Bart, it's a sacrifice I'm prepared to make. I don't need the prestige that comes with run-

111

ning in the race, but I do need the money from my job." Roger could see that the sparkle was gone from Lila's eyes. "Now, what was it you wanted to tell me?"

Roger's integrity was admirable, but Lila wanted nothing to do with it. Sacrifice was a word that wasn't in her vocabulary. She certainly hoped no one else knew about his job. "Oh, it was nothing important," Lila said, her party plans now ruined.

"Somehow I'm not surprised," Roger said, feeling both angry and hurt. "I realize you've just answered all my questions. See you around, Lila. I've got some people to talk to."

But the coach would have to wait, Roger thought as the warning bell rang. Forced to rely on his speed, he dashed down the hall and up the stairs to his first-period class, getting there with plenty of time to spare.

Later that morning, still carrying his sweat suit, Roger stood trembling before Coach Schultz. The white-haired coach was at his desk poring over a large ledger book. Without even looking up, he addressed his visitor. "Have a seat, Roger," he said, his voice showing a friendliness he seldom revealed to his students. "I was just looking over some records from around the state. Do you realize your qualifying time was the fourth-fastest mile ever run by a high schooler?"

Roger didn't acknowledge the question. "Coach, I have something to tell you."

"Of course you realize with a little practice you can improve on that mark. When am I going to see you out there, boy?" The coach looked up, the friendliness draining from his face.

"Oh, please, Coach Schultz, you just don't understand why I can't be at practice," Roger said. "And even worse, why I won't be able to run on Saturday."

"Did you sprain your ankle? Come down with viral pneumonia? Get an excuse from the president of the United States?" The coach's typical gruffness was back in full form. "Because those are about the only excuses I'd accept from you." The coach rose, and even though he was a fairly short man, he loomed over Roger, making the boy feel about as big as an ant—and just as powerless.

"It—it's none of those, sir," Roger said haltingly. "It's tearing me apart. I know how much I'm letting you and the school down. But you see, sir, I have a job that I can't afford to lose."

Coach Schultz relaxed visibly. "Is that all?" he said. "That's no problem, my boy."

"You don't understand, Coach. My boss—"

The coach cut him off. "A fella by the name of Pendergast, right?" Coach Schultz returned to his chair and faced Roger, who looked totally confused. "Talked to him this morning, as a matter of fact. He's a little fella, isn't he? Kind of like a weasel?"

Roger chuckled. "That's one way of putting it."

The coach nodded. "Could tell from his voice. Funny how even over the phone—"

"Excuse me, sir," Roger interrupted. "Are you telling me you called my boss this morning?"

"No, he called me. Wanted to let me know he wasn't going to stand in the way of you running in the Bart. He said he was going to let you come in an hour late the rest of the week and was giving you all day Saturday off."

"I don't believe it," Roger said, shaking his head. "That doesn't sound like Mr. Pendergast at all."

"Maybe you don't know him as well as you think. Did you realize he went to school with Jack Ralston? He knows how important the Bart is. When he heard you were eligible, he was surprised you hadn't gone to talk to him about it. You won't have any problems with him."

The unexpected news was slowly sinking in. "I can really run?" Roger said disbelievingly.

"I'm counting on you to," the coach warned.

Roger smiled. "Don't worry, sir. I'll be there," he said, his newfound excitement reflected in his voice. "Not only will I give Patman a run for his money—I might even break four minutes!"

"That's the spirit!"

Roger stood up. "I don't know how to thank you, sir. I'm very grateful."

"For what?"

"For explaining everything to Mr. Pendergast, of course."

"I didn't explain a thing to him. He already knew—and somehow he had a hunch you'd be coming in here today ready to back out of the race."

"Then who—?" Roger let the rest of the question hang in the air as he realized who his guardian angel was.

"I can't answer that, but someone's looking out for your interests. Now, can I expect to see you there?"

Roger's enthusiasm was boundless. "I'll be there after school," he promised. "And, Coach, I know you want to go out a winner. I intend to help you do it."

"Go out where? You putting me out to pasture, Roger?"

"Coach, we all know about it, how much pain you're in and how you're hanging in till after the race."

"What are you talking about, Roger?"

"Why, your retirement, sir. It's all over school how you're going to be leaving Sweet Valley after the race."

The coach scratched his head. "Maybe you'd

better sit down and tell me about this. As far as I'm concerned, I'm going nowhere."

Roger leaned against the desk. "You mean you're not sick?"

"Never been sick a day in my life. In fact, I had a checkup just last week. The doctor said I have the body of a thirty-year-old—and at my age that's pretty good. So where'd you hear I was leaving?"

"I don't remember exactly who was the first to tell me. But I heard you'd announced your retirement at the last board meeting."

The small office began to vibrate with the coach's laughter. "Is that what the kids are saying?" he asked, still laughing. "Someone out there's got a vivid imagination."

"I don't understand."

"I'm *not* sick, and I'm *not* leaving, Roger. I threw one of my usual tantrums at the board, threatening to quit if they didn't cough up funds for redoing the football field. I put on a show like that about once a year—and as usual it worked. I got the money I requested, and the board got to keep me on. Someone must have heard about the meeting and taken it too seriously." He began to chuckle again. "But how it got twisted into my impending demise sure beats me."

Roger smiled. "I'm so glad you're all right, sir," he said, rising. "And if it's OK with you, I'd still like to dedicate this race to you."

"If that's what it takes to make you run faster, it's fine with me," the coach said.

Roger walked out of the coach's office ready to believe in Santa Claus coming down the chimney—and in the Easter Bunny and the Tooth Fairy, too. True, he had his work cut out for him, but he felt as if a huge burden had been lifted from his shoulders. He now had the race and his job and even time to go to the dance afterward. He might not stand a chance of going with Lila, but somehow that didn't seem so important anymore.

Quickening his pace, he ran down the hall to the cafeteria. He had some unfinished business to attend to.

Ten

Too excited to eat, Roger bypassed the cafeteria line and headed out to the patio. Scanning the crowded tables, he spotted the person he wanted to see, the person he felt was most responsible for enabling him to run.

He ran up to Elizabeth Wakefield and gave her a big kiss. "Thanks a million, Liz," he said.

Todd Wilkins, sitting next to Elizabeth, gave him a funny look. "Hey buddy, that's my girl." He didn't seem really angry, though.

"Todd, that was merely a kiss of gratitude. Because of your girlfriend, I'm going to be able to run on Saturday."

"I never thought there was any question of that," Todd said.

"I'll explain later," Elizabeth told him. "Roger, how did you find out?"

"I just came from Coach Schultz's office." Roger took a seat opposite her. "He said someone spoke to Mr. Pendergast, and I figured it had to have been you."

"You're partially right. Actually, my father was the one who convinced him to give you the time off."

"It's funny," Roger continued. "I never figured him to be such a sports fan."

Elizabeth looked stunned. "Sports fan, hah. Did you know, Roger, that there's a state law that requires Mr. Pendergast to give you vacation time? Not to mention sick days. He had to give you the time off, as I'm sure Dad pointed out to him. Sometimes it pays to be a lawyer."

"I don't know how I'm going to thank your father," Roger said. "He really put himself on the line for me."

"Don't worry about it. He doesn't like Mr. Pendergast any more than you do. But if you want to do something for him, you can win on Saturday. My dad *is* a sports fan, and he's rooting for you all the way."

"We're all rooting for you, Roger," Todd said.

"But there's someone else you should be thanking," Elizabeth hastened to point out. "I wouldn't have known about your problem if it weren't for a certain somebody."

"Olivia." Roger whispered her name as he scanned the area around them. He spotted her sitting a few yards away, under a spruce tree, reading a book of poetry.

"I have a feeling she really cares about you," Elizabeth hinted.

"I'm beginning to realize it more and more," Roger said softly. "Uh, if you'll excuse me, Liz . . ."

"I understand, Roger," Elizabeth said. But almost before the words were out, Roger was heading toward the spruce.

When he got there he knelt down and lifted the book from Olivia's hands. "Any room for a dumb jock down here?"

"I don't see one around," she said.

"You're looking at him. Oh, Liv, I've been so stupid not to realize what's been staring me in the face for so long."

"What are you talking about?"

"You, Liv, and how much you really care about me. I mean, if it weren't for you, I wouldn't be able to run in the Bart. I don't know how to thank you."

"You're really going to be able to run? Oh, Roger, that's wonderful!" Olivia's smile brought out her loveliness. "I'm so glad for you, Roger," she said happily. "I hope you win."

"Will you be rooting for me?"

"Of course I will," she announced. "You don't think I'd root for anyone else, do you?"

"No," Roger said, throwing Elizabeth a yes-I-see-you're-right look. "How could I have missed it?" he asked.

"Missed what?" Olivia countered.

"The love in your eyes." Tentatively he reached for her hand, which she gave him willingly, and was pleasantly surprised by how good it felt. He squeezed it tenderly.

"If this is what jocks are like, I should have taken up an interest in sports a long time ago," she said.

Seeing that as a signal, Roger brushed his lips against her hand. "I've been so dumb, Liv. We're both pretty unconventional, and I guess I used to think we were friends more out of self-protection than anything else. But how could I have asked for someone more loyal to me than you? You've always been around to talk to whenever I needed it. You were there to cheer me up when I'd overhear someone making fun of me. You did it expecting nothing in return—except maybe a little friendship. Well, I'm ready to tell you that even though I may not have shown it until now, there's always been a little part of my heart that belonged to you. I'm ready to give you all of it if you're willing to accept it."

"You were never very good at poetry, Roger, but I accept," Olivia said. But she couldn't help adding, "What about Lila?"

Roger winced at the sound of the name. "All she wanted was to bask in my glory. She never cared for me at all."

"It must hurt," Olivia said, though greatly relieved Lila was no longer a threat. "When did you realize what she was doing?"

"This morning when I told her I wasn't running. Which reminds me—I want to catch Bruce before lunch is over and tell him he's got competition after all. I'm sure Lila's already told him about my dropping out of the race."

Olivia was suddenly struck with a thought. "Don't tell him, Roger."

"I've got to. The coach expects me to practice with him after school."

"Can you practice without him?" Olivia wondered, an idea brewing in her head even as she spoke.

Roger thought about it a moment. "I suppose I could," he told her, "but why should I?"

Olivia laid out her reasoning. "Lila thinks you're not running, correct?" Roger nodded. "By the end of the afternoon, the news will be all over school. Quite likely the other schools will hear about it, too. Talk it over with the coach. I'm sure he'll agree that pretending to keep you out of the race is good strategy. It'll catch the other schools off guard."

"But if I'm not supposed to be running, how can I show up on Saturday?"

"You'll still be officially entered. It'll only be a rumor that you're not. Then, right before the race, you can make a grand entrance, sort of like out-Bruce-ing Bruce Patman."

Roger appeared intrigued with the idea, but even more amazed by its source. "I never figured you to have an ounce of deception in you."

Olivia smiled, anticipating the look of shock on Lila's face when she saw Roger take the field on Saturday. "Let me just say that even the most honest person in the world feels the need for revenge every once in a while."

"I know what you mean," he said, recalling the derisive look on Bruce's face after the race trials. "I know exactly what you mean."

Sharing their secret, the two strode hand in hand across the campus lawn, counting the days until the race was set to start.

Jessica, too, was counting the days—with increasing dread. She had dropped all sorts of hints, but she still hadn't gotten Dennis to commit himself to taking her to the Bart dance—or anyplace else for that matter outside the immediate vicinity of the office. Lila's cancellation of her party hadn't helped matters, either. For one of the few times in her life, Jessica was at a total loss to explain a boy's behavior. It was almost as if Dennis were embarrassed to be seen in public with her.

Time having run out, she was forced to take a more direct approach. The night before the race, she got her chance, after she and Dennis had spent yet another evening alone in her father's office. "This is wonderful, Dennis," she whispered into his ear, her heart still pounding from his kisses.

"You really are terrific, Jess," he murmured, returning the compliment. "I've never known anyone like you."

Still nestled in the crook of his arm, she purred in her most tempting voice, "It sure is a shame to have to wait until Monday to do this again."

Dennis sighed uneasily. "Yeah," he agreed.

Jessica's voice hardened just a bit. "It doesn't have to be that way, Dennis."

"What do you mean?" he replied, a little too defensively. "I'm perfectly happy about the way things are going. Aren't you?"

"No, I'm not, Dennis, which is why I'm bringing this up. I get the feeling you're not being entirely straightforward with me."

Dennis cleared his throat. "Gee, what makes you say that?"

Jessica thought he sounded nervous. Now she was certain he was hiding something. Part of her didn't want to find out what it was, but the more practical side of her knew the time had come to get to the bottom of things. "I don't know about you, but I haven't made any plans for the weekend."

"What about the Bart dance? You've been talking about it all week."

Jessica stiffened. Did he really think she'd go without him? "Why do you think I've mentioned it? Because I like hearing the sound of my voice against these walls? I wanted *you* to ask me, dummy!" She turned to face him. "But since you haven't, I see I'll have to do the job myself." Deftly switching gears, she lowered her voice and said seductively, "Dennis Creighton, will you take me to the Bart dance tomorrow night?"

Dennis lowered his head. He seemed embarrassed. "I—I can't," he said. All the self-assurance was gone from his voice.

Jessica couldn't believe it. Enraged, she jumped from the sofa where the two of them had been sitting and leaned against the wall on the opposite side of the room. "And why not?" she demanded. "Don't your parents let you out of the house on Saturday nights?"

"Sure . . ." he began weakly.

"Oh, I see," Jessica continued, answering for him. "It's all so perfectly clear I should have suspected it a long time ago." She began to pace back and forth across the outer office. "There's another girl, right? Your weekend sweetie, who's away during the rest of the week. And so poor Dennis, who was all alone and feeling sorry for himself, had to find someone else to keep him occupied. And who should come along but sweet, unsuspecting little old me." Jessica's voice chilled. "Well, you can forget about it because I won't stand for it a second longer." She stormed to the closet and grabbed her pocketbook and sweater.

125

She was reaching for the door handle when Dennis rose and shouted, "Stop!"

Jessica halted in her tracks. "What else could you *possibly* have to say to me?" she hissed.

"Hear me out, please," Dennis begged. "I know you're probably going to walk out of here anyway, but maybe you won't hate me as much after you hear what I've got to tell you."

"I can't imagine it'll make a difference," she said. Nevertheless, she walked back to the sofa and lowered herself onto one of the arms. "But go ahead. Shoot."

Dennis fidgeted with the buttons on his shirt, trying to decide where to begin. "I like you, Jess. Really, I do. Believe me, you're the only girl in my life."

"But you can't stand the idea of hanging out with me in public," Jessica spat. "What's the matter? Not good enough for you or something?"

"Don't be silly, Jess. Please let me go on," Dennis pleaded. "I'd love to take you out. To the dance or to the beach or whatever. But I can't. See . . . I told you I had a car, but I don't."

Jessica rolled her eyes. "Is that all?" she exclaimed. "That's no big deal. Can't you borrow your dad's?"

"No," he said.

Jessica thought a moment. She didn't like having to do this, but if it was the only way she could get Dennis to the dance. . . . "I could pick you up in my car, and then you could drive us—"

Dennis shook his head. "No, you don't understand. Not only don't I have a car, I don't have a driver's license. I just turned fifteen."

"Oh." Jessica was at a rare loss for words. For a long time she just stared at him, looking at the boy she'd assumed was close to eighteen in a completely new light. "That does change things, doesn't it?"

"I hope you don't hate me," Dennis said timidly, his age clearly showing through his crumbled facade of confidence.

"How did you think you could get away with it?" Jessica asked.

"I know how you must feel, a girl like you finding out she's been hanging out with a kid—especially when you thought I was much older. I realized you'd dump me if I told you the truth, so I kept my mouth shut. I figured if I could hide my age until I got my learner's permit, it might make a difference. If it still matters to you," he added hopefully, "I start driver's ed in two months."

Jessica took in Dennis's words with conflicting emotions. She liked him. She really did. And part of her still wanted Dennis at her side during the Bart dance. But what would everyone say when they found out her date wasn't even old enough to drive? She could just picture the look on Lila's face. Besides, Dennis had

had the nerve to keep the truth from her all these weeks.

Jessica Wakefield was the picture of innocence wronged. Keeping her voice hard, she addressed Dennis for the last time. "It's too late for true confessions," she told him. "Goodbye, Dennis." Quickly she ran for the elevator, hoping it would arrive before Dennis had a chance to catch up to her—and see the tears welling in her eyes.

———

Eleven

No one could have asked for a finer day for the thirty-first running of the Bart. Marshmallow-white clouds dotted the sky, keeping the temperature from rising too high. A slight breeze blew in from the ocean, making the air comfortable for the crowds pouring into the Sweet Valley College stadium.

The multitiered stands were divided into rooting sections for the five participating schools. The Sweet Valley High contingent was situated in one of the areas closest to the field. Several signs reading We Love You Bruce and Tony were being unfurled, although a few diehards who hadn't believed the rumor that Roger had dropped out of the race also held up banners with his name on them.

Elizabeth and Todd found seats toward the top of the Sweet Valley section. Todd scanned the faces below them and was surprised to see

Jessica along with the other cheerleaders. "I thought she was married to that job of hers these days," he noted.

"She quit, Todd," Elizabeth told him.

"The law not her cup of tea?" From the way he said it, he made it clear that he found Jessica's decision not at all surprising.

"I'm not convinced it ever was," Elizabeth said. "The only reason she worked as long as she did was because of a guy."

"I should have suspected there was a guy involved. There always seems to be." Todd raised an eyebrow. "What happened? Did he try to take advantage of her?"

Elizabeth shook her head. "Not in the way you think." Elizabeth related Jessica's version of what had happened the night before.

"And of course your twin can't stand the thought of being with a younger man," Todd concluded.

Elizabeth sighed, remembering the sadness she'd heard in Jessica's voice. "I think she really liked him, Todd. But Jess considers being fifteen a handicap no boy could ever overcome. She hasn't had the best of luck with guys lately, and she feels a lot of people around here might conclude she was so desperate for someone that she settled for a younger guy. Imagine how humiliated she'd feel chauffeuring him around everywhere." Elizabeth shook her head, her blond ponytail swinging from one shoulder to the other. "It's a shame, though. I think if it had happened to me, I would have said the heck with what anyone says and gone out with him anyway."

"I'll keep that in mind the next time I see you snuggling up to a ninth grader," Todd kidded.

Elizabeth grabbed Todd's hand and squeezed it playfully. "I wouldn't worry about it too much if I were you. But seriously, Todd, I feel bad for Jess. She seemed pretty upset this morning."

"Well, I wouldn't waste my time feeling sorry for your sister," Todd said. "Knowing Jessica, she'll be after someone else before the day's out."

Dressed in her red and white uniform, Jessica was in the middle of a last-minute practice with her squad before the bulk of the crowd arrived. She figured the cheering would keep her busy— busy enough, she hoped, to recover from the latest disappointment in her life. As the stands began to fill up, she felt her spirits rise. With five high schools' worth of boys to feast her eyes on, she realized that getting Dennis Creighton out of her system would be much easier than she'd thought.

Standing as close to Jessica as possible was Annie Whitman, wearing a minidress short enough to make her a girl watcher's delight. But boys were the farthest thing from Annie's mind this morning. All her energy was focused on Jessica and the other cheerleaders as they went through their routines, and she even tried running through some of the motions herself. Tryouts for the cheerleading squad were coming up soon, and Annie wanted to be sure she had all the moves down perfectly. Several times she tried to get Jessica's attention, but Jessica either didn't hear her or pretended not to.

On the field, Coach Schultz was giving a final pep talk to Bruce Patman and Tony Esteban. Then, looking supremely confident, Bruce took off his warm-up suit and headed toward the starting line. Because of the number of boys in competition, the race was to be run in heats, and he was one of the participants in the first heat. The top three finishers of both heats would then square off in the final race, and the winner would be awarded the silver trophy displayed on the judges' table—and the scholarship to Sweet Valley College.

Anticipation was in the air. Jessica led the Sweet Valley crowd in the chant, "Go, Bruce, go." With Roger apparently out of the picture, Bruce was Sweet Valley's only real hope for victory, and all eyes were on him.

That was exactly the way he liked it. The dark-haired boy smiled to his fans and even waved as he did a few jogging steps for the crowd.

"Look at that guy," Todd said disgustedly to

Elizabeth, "playing to the crowd as usual. He's going to burn himself up."

"I don't know," Elizabeth said. "I really think he wants to win this one. You know how big his ego can be."

"Well, we'll see soon enough. They're getting ready to start."

There were the obligatory introductions and the playing of the national anthem before the first race got under way. The stadium was eerily silent as the main judge raised his starter's pistol in the air. "On your mark, get set, go!"

The runners were off. Having learned a lesson from his race with Roger, Bruce held back at first, letting Joe Epson, one of the runners from El Carro High, fly into the lead. The coach had told him that the boy was known for fast starts but that his staying power was questionable. So Bruce concentrated on keeping his stamina and remaining just far enough behind Epson to make the other boy feel overconfident. He spent the early part of the race jockeying for second with two other boys. It was exactly where he wanted to be.

By the half-mile mark, however, it had obviously become a two person race. The other boys, now visibly tiring, began to drift farther behind the leaders. One boy from Palisades High, the apparent victim of a muscle pull, even had to drop out, much to the disappointment of his school.

Bruce finally made his move on the final lap. Coming into the final turn, he bore down as hard as he could, and with a burst of reserved speed flashed by Joe Epson. Bruce finished a good three seconds ahead of him and fell into the arms of his teammate Tony as the crowd roared its approval.

"You made it, amigo," Tony congratulated him.

Still puffing, Bruce said, "It's only the beginning. I expect to see you running next to me in the finals. Go to it, Esteban."

Because Tony was not expected to do well, the enthusiasm in the Sweet Valley stands for the second heat was considerably weaker. If it hadn't been for the announcement over the loudspeaker, many of the students might not even have realized their star miler was running after all.

". . . and in lane seven is Roger Barrett from Sweet Valley High."

All eyes focused on the slender boy, who cut a handsome figure dressed in a brand-new pair of red running shorts with the white high school tank top. It was quite a change from the ragged-looking figure who'd run that first race.

"I don't know how he did it," Lila said to one of her sorority friends, conveniently taking over once again as Roger's self-appointed number-one fan. "But doesn't he look great? You know, I bet he planned this whole ruse just to shock the other schools. Imagine coming up with that dumb story about a job and a mean boss." She let out a laugh.

Elizabeth, overhearing the whole thing, was astonished at how conniving Lila could be when she put her mind to it.

"There's still time to plan that party after all," Lila said aloud. "After this race I'll call my father and have him get our cook to whip up a few things. Oh, it's going to be great!"

"Excuse me, Lila." Elizabeth turned around. "I couldn't help overhearing. You say the party's on again?"

Lila struck a pose. "It was so heartless of me to plan to do something for the coach and then decide to drop it for a silly little reason. No one else is doing a tribute, so it's left to me."

"Gee, I hate to break this to you, Lila, but Coach Schultz isn't leaving the school. All those rumors going around about him are false."

"Oh, you're just making that up, Liz. Can't you see how tired the man looks? It's obvious he's sick."

"Lila, what everyone around school has failed to notice recently is that the coach has *always* looked tired. Really, he's in great shape. You'll read all about it in next week's *Oracle*."

"Hmmph," Lila snorted. "Well, I'll have the party anyway. This time the party's going to be in honor of Roger. A victory party."

135

"What makes you so sure he's going to win?" Elizabeth asked.

"Where's your faith, Liz? Of course he is! That guy can do anything," she said, her admiration of him back in full force. "Just look at that bod." She sighed.

"A few days ago, you didn't want to have anything to do with him."

"Oh, that," she said, nonchalantly, dismissing her abrupt rejection of him. "I'm sure Roger knows I didn't mean anything by it—especially since he's the one who forced the issue, coming up with that story about not being able to run. How else was I supposed to react?"

Elizabeth thought a moment before answering, then realized that Lila probably didn't know any other way. "All I can tell you, Lila, is don't be surprised if Roger decides not to show up." She was going to say something about Olivia, but her attention was diverted to the track and the start of the second heat. Standing next to each other, Roger and Tony held up their joined arms in unity and wished each other luck.

Then they took their marks. Both boys sat comfortably back in the pack for the first part of the race, letting the top miler from Springbrook High set the pace. But by the two-thirds mark, Roger began to find the pace too slow and advanced into the lead himself, where he remained until he crossed the finish line. The big surprise of the race was Tony, who finished third and

thus ensured that all three Sweet Valley quali-
fiers would be running in the final.

The crowd went wild. Jessica was convinced
she'd lose her voice by the end of the afternoon
but kept right on cheering anyway. Even Annie
Whitman had managed to cheer her heart out
in the bleachers, wishing all the time that she
were down there with the squad.

Yet everyone had reserved a little extra for
the final race, the most important one of all.
The Sweet Valley High runners were lined up
in lanes one, two, and three. In lane four was
Joe Epson, the speedster from El Carro, who
sneered derisively at Bruce, the boy who'd run
him out of first place in the first heat.

"You're not going to do it to me again, Mr.
Big Shot," the boy declared.

"You're in for a big surprise, then," Bruce
shot back, " 'cause that's exactly what I intend
to do."

"That's what you think," Joe hissed.

"Listen, buddy, if I were you, I'd give a little
thought to this guy over here, too," he said,
pointing to Roger.

"Oh, him." Joe dismissed Roger with a snort.
"There's no way he could run that fast twice in
one day. He's probably burned himself out."

Bruce just smiled. He found himself having
come to a grudging admiration for Roger's
running, if not for Roger himself. He was still

trying to get over the deception both Roger and the coach had pulled on him.

But there was no time to think about it. The final heat was about to begin. Bruce set his eyes on the track ahead of him and the glory that would be his when he stepped first across the finish line.

Roger, too, was focusing all his attention on the path ahead. He'd been able to catch everyone by surprise in the first heat, but now every runner on the track would be setting his sights on beating him. Did he have enough left inside to pull out another victory? he wondered.

The answer would be clear in less than five minutes. The starting gun went off, and from then on the pounding sound of feet was all Roger could concentrate on. Bruce was running with him stride for stride, apparently deciding that if he couldn't beat him, he'd join him as long as he could. Tony was right up with them, running faster than he ever had in his life. Joe Epson was close behind, although leading them all was one of the runners from Springbrook.

The pace was very fast, faster than Roger was accustomed to and much faster than he desired. It was sapping his strength, and he wasn't sure he could keep it up, let alone have enough left over for victory.

All he could do was try. Bearing down harder, he moved several steps ahead of Bruce. Tony, he realized, was already fading, as was the other runner from Springbrook High. Joe, the boy from El Carro, was right there alongside Bruce.

Then, out the corner of his eye, Roger noticed that something had happened. Bruce was no longer anywhere near him. Rumblings from the stadium made him aware that something had gone wrong. All he knew was that Joe Epson had moved up beside him, a smug sneer on his face.

About half a lap back, Bruce lay on the track, stinging from the fall he took when he was tripped. He was so far back now that he stood no chance of winning, but a gritty determination forced him to get up and continue racing. It was a move the crowd loved, as was evident from the huge cheer that went up as soon as Bruce picked up his pace.

Roger didn't know why everyone was cheering, but the noise, coupled with the pressure he felt from Epson, spurred him on. Up ahead, the boy from Springbrook was slowing down a little; with luck, he was tiring. Roger felt it was time to make his move. Pushing harder, he willed himself forward and felt the wind blast a little stronger against his face. Soon he was neck and neck with the Springbrook boy and about to head into the lead.

But Joe was right with him. For half a lap the two vied for the lead. With the finish line approaching rapidly, there wasn't time for fancy strategy. All Roger could do was run as fast as humanly possible. Using every ounce of energy and calling on a reserve he didn't even know he had, he burst ahead and finished a good three or four strides in front of the other boy.

He ran off the track, winding down and then collapsing on the soft grass infield. It felt so good to stop, he'd momentarily forgotten what his accomplishment meant.

But plenty of others were ready to remind him. The first to come to him were his teammates Bruce and Tony, who lifted him high above the approaching crowd. They let him down only during the presentation of the trophy and the scholarship.

"I can't think of a more deserving boy for this honor," Coach Schultz said, handing him the certificate detailing the scholarship award. "Let's all give a big hand to the boy of the hour, Roger Barrett." The coach paused as everyone, even Sweet Valley's rivals, gave Roger a standing ovation. When the fervor died down, the coach raised his hands in the air, indicating he wanted their attention again. "We have the official time for the race. Roger came in at three minutes, fifty-nine point eight seconds. A new Bart record!"

Roger had had plenty to cry about during his

life, but now, for the first time, he felt his eyes moisten with tears of joy. Without shame he continued to let the tears flow as he rode on the biggest high of his life.

Twelve

Roger was still standing at the winner's podium as the crowd began filing slowly out of the stadium. While it was true that he was savoring his moment of glory as long as he could, he was also using the vantage point to try to find Olivia.

Unable to do so, he stepped off the platform and began walking toward the stadium bleachers. A large crowd of Sweet Valley faithfuls began to surround him.

"I knew you could do it, Roger." The compliment came from Mr. Pendergast, who broke through the crowd to shake the boy's hand. Roger was surprised he'd even come to the race. Maybe the guy had a soft spot after all. "Of course I expect to see you back at work on Monday."

"Of course," Roger grumbled. In an attempt to lose his boss in the crowd, he turned around—

only to find himself eyeball to eyeball with Lila.

"Congratulations, Roger! I'm so proud of you."
She was looking at him in the same adoring
fashion as after the qualifying race. "I always
knew you'd win," she gushed, making a great
display of kissing him full and hard on the lips.
"I never lost faith in you. Never."

Roger wanted to ask her where her faith was
when he'd confessed he couldn't afford to run,
but he saw no point in showing the crowd
that she was lying. It didn't matter anymore,
anyway.

Lila continued to chatter away as she followed him across the infield. "I've taken the
liberty of inviting some of my closest friends to
a party in your honor," she told him. "It starts
at five. At my place. And don't forget to bring
your bathing suit. You might as well bring your
clothes for the dance, too. There's plenty of
room to change."

Roger stopped walking and looked at her with
disgust. She was so sure of herself, so posi-
tively sure that there was nothing in the world
he'd rather do than go to a stupid party at her
pool. "Sorry, Lila. I can't make it."

Her jaw dropped. "What can you be doing
that's more important?" she asked indignantly.

"Frankly, it's none of your business," he said.
The experiences of the past week had made
him realize what kind of values were truly important to him. And they didn't always come

with big price tags. Lila wasn't worth another instant of his time. "I'll see you later." He left her standing amid the other well-wishers.

Pulling himself away from the crowd, he headed toward the stadium stands. There, sitting alone, was Olivia. He took the small girl in his arms and twirled her in the air. "We did it!" he shouted, lowering her to give her a kiss.

"What do you mean, we?" she said. "That was you out there, running your heart out. How do you feel?"

"Never better," he said. "And I couldn't have done it all without you. I thought you knew that."

"I do," she said, grinning. "But I like to hear it anyway."

"How come you weren't out there?" he asked, pointing to the crowd on the infield.

"Crowds bother me. I was content to wait. My patience is unlimited," she said.

"I hope you were patient enough not to have made plans for this evening. I can't think of anyone I'd rather spend it with than you."

"What about your fans?" she asked.

"They wouldn't have cared a thing about me if I'd lost," he said. "But I have a pretty good hunch you'd still have been sitting here waiting for me. Am I right?"

Shyly she nodded.

"I know it's taken me a while, but I've finally come to realize who my true friends are." He kissed her softly on the forehead. Then he flashed a wicked grin. "That was a kiss of friendship. Now I'll show you the kiss I really want to give you." Lowering his mouth over hers, he pressed firmly yet tenderly on her lips. She responded in kind, letting him know his affection was definitely not one-sided.

It didn't go unnoticed. Elizabeth and Todd had been following Roger in an effort to congratulate him, but now they moved away discreetly. "Maybe we'll see him at the dance," Elizabeth said softly.

"I don't know, Liz. The way those two are going at it, I wouldn't be surprised if we found them still here on Monday morning."

Elizabeth chuckled. "If you don't mind, I'm going to catch up with Jessica and head home with her. I think she needs the company. See you tonight."

Elizabeth found Jessica a few minutes later, walking casually toward the parking lot with Cara Walker. "Mind if I come along with you?" she asked.

"Liz, we were just talking about Roger and Olivia. I can't believe that boy's passing up Lila for her." Jessica looked shocked. "Did you see them back there?"

"Yes, but I've known about them for a couple of days now. I knew Roger was running, too."

"And you didn't tell me?" Jessica sounded deeply hurt.

Cara punched her friend lightly on the shoulder. "Come on, Jess. Liz knows you'd have told the whole school. It would have spoiled everything."

"Not you, too?" Jessica cried. But she wasn't really hurt. "I'd have killed to have gotten a look at Lila's face when she saw them," Jessica went on. "But I couldn't find her anyplace."

"She's probably recovering in private," Elizabeth said. "By tonight I'm sure she'll be calling him Bugs again and putting him down."

"But the rest of us won't be laughing anymore," Jessica said. "He's not such a bad guy when you get right down to it—though *I'd* never want to go out with him." She giggled.

"It's good to see you smiling," Elizabeth said, "after what happened last night."

Cara cut her off. "Jess, didn't you tell Liz about Kevin?"

"Kevin who?" Elizabeth asked.

"My date for the dance tonight," Jessica said casually. "During the break between races, one of the Springbrook cheerleaders—Kevin Borden—came over to compliment me on a cheer. Well, one thing led to another, and—"

"And he asked you out," Elizabeth finished her sister's sentence. "Somehow I knew it wouldn't take you long to get over Dennis."

"Dennis who?" Jessica said with another giggle.

"Jessica! There you are!" Annie Whitman tugged at Jessica's uniform and practically had

146

to stand in front of her to get her to stop. "I tried to get your attention earlier, but I guess you couldn't hear me with all that noise."

"I guess not," Jessica said, annoyed that she hadn't been totally successful in avoiding the sexy sophomore. She continued to walk, and Annie had no choice but to walk with her.

"You look busy, so I won't keep you," Annie said. "I just want to let you know I'm free to try out for the cheerleading squad."

"According to the school rules everyone is," Jessica had to admit. *Even easy girls like you*, she almost added.

"Not if you're flunking. I was in trouble with two of my classes but not anymore. Are there going to be practice sessions before the tryouts?"

Jessica sighed. "Yes, Annie. The details will be in the next issue of *The Oracle*." *How do I get rid of this girl?* she wondered.

"Great. I know all the cheers by heart, but there are a couple of steps I'm a little unsure of." She moved ahead of the twins and Cara. "Like I said, I don't want to keep you. See you at tryouts." Waving goodbye, she walked off toward the bus stop.

"Good luck, Annie," Elizabeth called after her.

"Why'd you say that?" Jessica asked her sister.

"I like to see hard work rewarded," she answered. "It paid off for Roger today. It'd be nice if the same thing happened to Annie."

147

"Why?" Jessica said angrily. "So she could use her cheerleading uniform as an added lure for the boys?"

"Annie's not like that," Elizabeth said.

Jessica snorted. "Where have you been, big sister? On Jupiter? That girl's got to hold the school record for most dates! If 'date' is the right word for what Annie does."

"I didn't know you were keeping track," Elizabeth noted.

"I keep my eye on every girl who expresses an interest in joining the squad," Jessica said. "Every single cheerleader is a public representative of our school, and it's my job to make sure they're deserving of the honor."

"And you think Annie's not deserving?" Elizabeth asked.

"Think, nothing! I *know* that girl is just a whole lot of bad news," Jessica declared.

Elizabeth shook her head. It was clear that Annie was going to have trouble with her sister. "But if she knows all the cheers and does them well, you've got to take her, don't you?"

Jessica stopped and put her hands on her hips. "Liz, I don't have to do anything I don't want to do. But I'm willing to bet anything she chickens out when it comes time for tryouts." Jessica chuckled. "At least she should if she knows what's good for her."

Annie was really in for it, Elizabeth fretted, recognizing that hard tone in Jessica's voice.

She'd sneaked around the rules once to deny membership in her sorority to a girl she didn't like, so it wouldn't be surprising if she did something similar to Annie when it came to the cheerleading squad. Elizabeth saw nothing but trouble ahead for the shapely, unsuspecting Annie Whitman. Big trouble.

What trouble is in store for Annie? Find out in Sweet Valley High #10, WRONG KIND OF GIRL.

☐	25143	**POWER PLAY #4**	$2.50
☐	25043	**ALL NIGHT LONG #5**	$2.50
☐	25105	**DANGEROUS LOVE #6**	$2.50
☐	25106	**DEAR SISTER #7**	$2.50
☐	25092	**HEARTBREAKER #8**	$2.50
☐	25026	**RACING HEARTS #9**	$2.50
☐	25016	**WRONG KIND OF GIRL #10**	$2.50
☐	25046	**TOO GOOD TO BE TRUE #11**	$2.50
☐	25035	**WHEN LOVE DIES #12**	$2.50
☐	24524	**KIDNAPPED #13**	$2.25
☐	24531	**DECEPTIONS #14**	$2.50
☐	24582	**PROMISES #15**	$2.50
☐	24672	**RAGS TO RICHES #16**	$2.50
☐	24723	**LOVE LETTERS #17**	$2.50
☐	24825	**HEAD OVER HEELS #18**	$2.50
☐	24893	**SHOWDOWN #19**	$2.50
☐	24947	**CRASH LANDING! #20**	$2.50

Prices and availability subject to change without notice.

Buy them at your local bookstore or use this handy coupon for ordering:

SWEET DREAMS are fresh, fun and exciting,—alive with the flavor of the contemporary teen scene—the joy and doubt of *first love*. If you've missed any SWEET DREAMS titles, from #1 to #100, then you're missing out on *your* kind of stories, written about people like *you*!

☐	24837	**DAY DREAMER #32** Janet Quin-Harkin	$2.25
☐	24336	**FORBIDDEN LOVE #35** Marian Woodruff	$2.25
☐	24338	**SUMMER DREAMS #36** Barbara Conklin	$2.25
☐	24340	**FIRST LOVE #39** Debra Spector	$2.25
☐	24838	**THE TRUTH ABOUT ME AND BOBBY V. #41** Janetta Johns	$2.25
☐	24341	**DREAM PROM #45** Margaret Burman	$2.25
☐	24688	**SECRET ADMIRER #81** Debra Spector	$2.25
☐	24383	**HEY, GOOD LOOKING #82** Jane Polcovar	$2.25
☐	24823	**LOVE BY THE BOOK #83** Anne Park	$2.25
☐	24718	**THE LAST WORD #84** Susan Blake	$2.25
☐	24890	**THE BOY SHE LEFT BEHIND #85** Suzanne Rand	$2.25
☐	24945	**QUESTIONS OF LOVE #86** Rosemary Vernon	$2.25
☐	24824	**PROGRAMMED FOR LOVE #87** Marion Crane	$2.25
☐	24891	**WRONG KIND OF BOY #88** Shannon Blair	$2.25
☐	24946	**101 WAYS TO MEET MR. RIGHT #89** Janet Quin-Harkin	$2.25
☐	24992	**TWO'S A CROWD #90** Diana Gregory	$2.25
☐	25070	**THE LOVE HUNT #91** Yvonne Green	$2.25
☐	25131	**KISS & TELL #92** Janet Quin-Harkin	$2.25
☐	25071	**THE GREAT BOY CHASE #93** Janet Quin-Harkin	$2.25
☐	25132	**SECOND CHANCES #94** Nancy Levinso	$2.25
☐	25178	**NO STRINGS ATTACHED #95** Eileen Hehl	$2.25
☐	25179	**FIRST, LAST, AND ALWAYS #96** Barbara Conklin	$2.25

Prices and availability subject to change without notice.

Special Offer
Buy a Bantam Book
for only 50¢.

Now you can order the exciting books you've been wanting to read straight from Bantam's latest listing of hundreds of titles. *And* this special offer gives you the opportunity to purchase a Bantam book for only 50¢. Here's how:

By ordering any five books at the regular price per order, you can also choose any other single book listed (up to $4.95 value) for only 50¢. Some restrictions do apply, so for further details send for Bantam's listing of titles today.

Just send us your name and address and we'll send you Bantam Book's SHOP AT HOME CATALOG!